TENDER PURDY

Tender Answers the Call

RICHARD P. HARRINGTON

Tender Purdy: Tender Answers the Call
Copyright © 2023 Richard P. Harrington

Produced and printed by Stillwater River Publications. All rights reserved. Written and produced in the United States of America. This book may not be reproduced or sold in any form without the expressed, written permission of the author(s) and publisher.

Visit our website at
www.StillwaterPress.com
for more information.

First Stillwater River Publications Edition

ISBN: 978-1-960505-58-3

Library of Congress Control Number: 2023916531

1 2 3 4 5 6 7 8 9 10

Written by Richard P. Harrington.
Cover illustration by Sheri Harrington.
Edited by Esther Porwoll.
Published by Stillwater River Publications,
West Warwick, RI, USA.

Scripture quotations from the
English Standard Bible, copyright © 2001 Crossway,
a publishing ministry of Good New Publishers.
Used with permission. All rights reserved.

The views and opinions expressed
in this book are solely those of the author(s)
and do not necessarily reflect the views
and opinions of the publisher.

To my Lord and Savior, Jesus Christ.

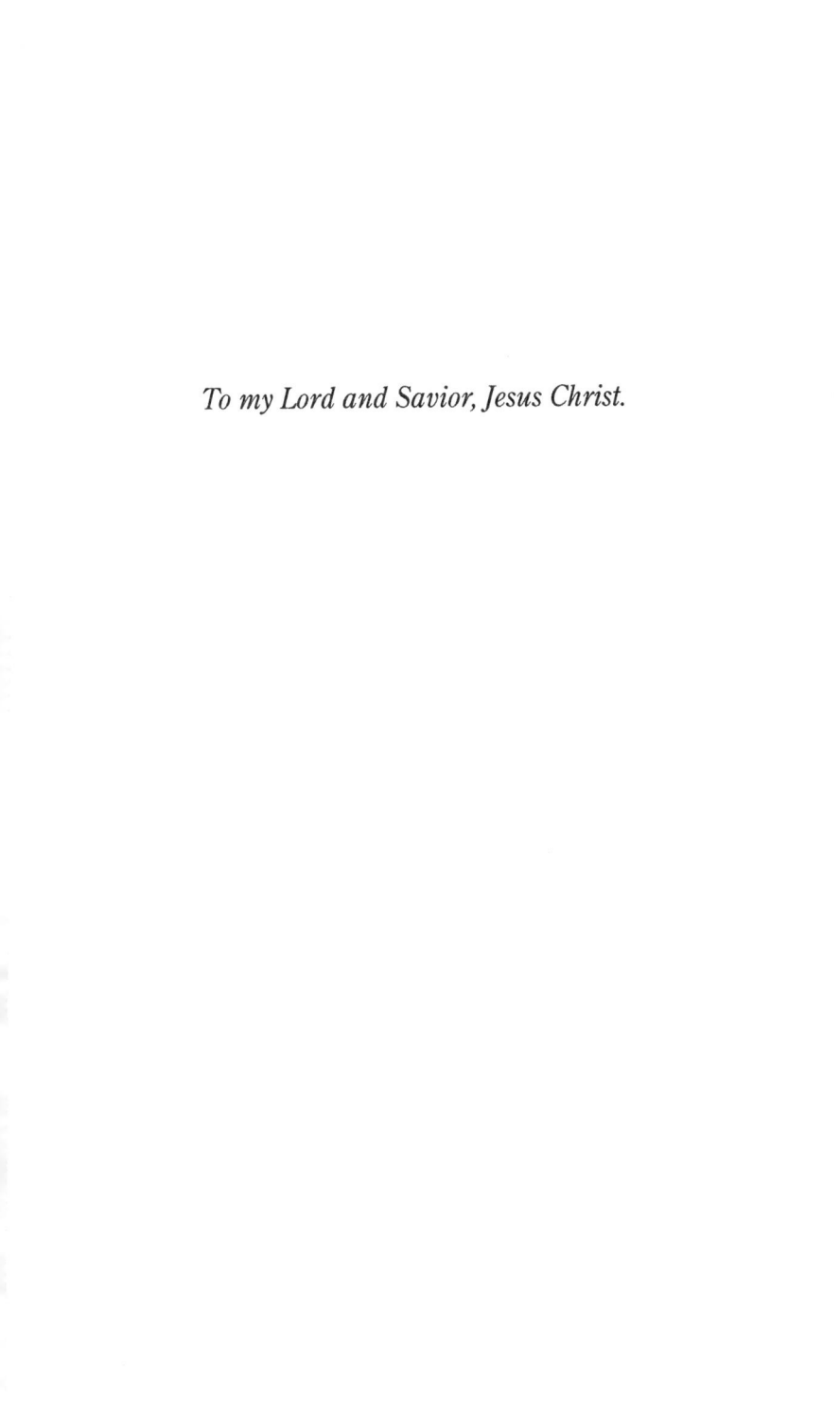

Table of Contents

1. Elaine Goes to College 1
2. The Wedding 31
3. Duty Calls 36
4. Tender Picks Her Parents 55
5. A Decision to Make. 65
6. Tender Makes New Friends 99
7. Tender Is Needed. 113
8. FBI Director Lance 128
9. Tender and the Mysterious Cold Case . 136
10. The Real Estate Murders. 155
11. This Hits Home 167
12. Sister Mary Ellen Needs Help 172
13. Where Are the Sixty? 199
14. Where Is Victory Smith? 234

    About the Author *241*

ONE

Elaine Goes to College

Hello, my name is Elaine. When I was a newborn, I was dropped off at an orphanage in Lincoln, North Dakota. Only a piece of paper was in the basket when they found me. It read, "Her first name is Elaine. Please find her a last name." Throughout my childhood, my only hope and prayer was that someone would show up and claim me, but that was never the case. Not many of us were adopted—only a few lucky ones.

I grew up at St. Paul's School for Girls. The nuns were always kind and took great care of me, but not knowing my real last name or birthday bothered me growing up. I was given "Smith" as my last name when I was dropped off. "Elaine Smith" sounded nice, but it never really felt right. Since they did not know when I was born, the nuns used the day of my arrival for my birthday: July 15, 1937. Every year, when it came to my birthday, I was excited but also sad, because it reminded me of the day I was dropped off at the orphanage.

The day finally came when I needed to say goodbye to Sister Mary Ellen, my good friends, and all the staff that I had come to love. As I listened to her tell me about how I was one of her favorite children, my mind kept wandering to all the other little girls still here. Would I ever have a little girl of my own? I wanted to give a child all the love of a family. Sister Mary Ellen asked me to always look for ways to help someone else that may have had similar life circumstances as I had growing up here. For the first time since my arrival, Sister Mary Ellen gave me a hug, and surprised me by telling me she loved me, we both cried, and I told her I loved her and that I was scared. She took me by the shoulders, "Elaine Smith you are going to go and make a change in this world, make me proud." As I departed with just one duffel bag I kept looking back as she kept waving to me until I was out of sight. I boarded a bus to Bismarck, North Dakota and even though it was a three-hour ride, my mind kept thinking back to my 18 years at Saint Paul's School for Girls.

Tender Answers the Call

I graduated with honors from St. Paul's in 1955, and I immediately enrolled in the two-year criminal justice program at Bismarck State College. I have always found police work so exciting. Growing up, I often wondered if one of my parents was involved in police work and was perhaps killed in the line of duty. I think that could be what sparked my interest in studying criminal justice. When I discovered that Bismarck State College offered a free education to any student that agreed to stay in North Dakota and work in public service for a period of five years after graduation, I was thrilled. North Dakota was the only place that I could ever imagine living. It has always felt like home to me.

The first day of school was chaotic. It was a good thing that the campus was small, because the whole first day, I was running all over the place. I rushed to the bookstore to buy my books before they sold out, got lost several times looking for my dorm room, and finally struggled to unpack my duffel bag and organize my belongings in the tiny room. Then my roommates arrived.

Linda Hope was tall with brown hair, brown eyes, a confident face, and a great smile. She was studying to be an attorney. I quickly discovered that she loved to talk, and her confidence made her very popular. She had a date almost every weekend. My other roommate, Joann Simpson, was just the opposite of Linda. She was also pretty, petite with blond hair and blue eyes, and was one of the prettiest girls on campus. But unlike Linda, she was very quiet, and she told me that she had attended a one room school and was a little overwhelmed by campus life. At first, Joann and I spent most weekends in our dorm, reading or listening to music. We got along perfectly, and I discovered that my new friend had a great sense of humor. But it wasn't long before Linda decided it was time to break Joann and I out of our shells, and she convinced us to hang out with her and her group of friends. Neither Joann nor I had much experience talking to boys, but Linda's friends were very nice and easy to chat with.

I dated a few guys that year, but my longest relationship was only six weeks. Joann, however, found someone very special. His name was Michael Wood, and he was from Bismarck. He was short, with spiky black hair and beautiful hazel eyes. He was one of the most intelligent people I have ever met. He and Joann hit it off right from the very first date. Linda and I started to see less and less of Joann. I was a little envious of her; she seemed so happy. I enjoyed going out with boys and getting to know them as friends, but that's all they were. None of them made me feel the way I'd read about in books. I asked Joann how she knew she was in love with Michael, and all she would say was that she felt incredible when she was around him. That was not very helpful.

On the other hand, Linda fell in and out of love with every boy she went out with. We used to tease her about it. All that changed when she met Roger Lake from Fargo, North Dakota. He was tall, with a sharp jaw, bold brown eyes, and curly light brown hair, and he was completely different to the outgoing, voluble boys she usually went out with. He was the strong, silent type, and very serious. Linda came back from their first date looking like she'd been struck by lightning. She was completely smitten and terrified that she hadn't made a good impression. Apparently, Roger had let her babble on and on and had said very little. As time went on, though, it became apparent that Roger was smitten as well. Although they were opposites, they complemented each other perfectly.

Before I knew it my first year was ending. It wasn't all fun and games; I had studied very hard and was so proud to discover I had made the Dean's list. To earn my free attendance, I had to stay on campus and work for the college as part of the on-campus security detail. I was thrilled to have a chance to get some hands-on experience in my major, and the stipend of twenty dollars every other week was a great bonus. For the first time, I was able to buy myself some nice clothes.

The summer ended, and along came fall, with the start of my second and final year in criminal justice. I wondered what was in store for my future. I worried about where I would work, and whether there was a town in North Dakota that would hire a female police officer.

The first day was nearly as frantic as it was my first year, but I was happy I could move back into the same dorm as the previous year and with the same roommates. I could barely contain my happiness as I greeted my two special friends with a big hug. We all started to talk at once, and then we all started giggling until Linda was finally able to make herself heard.

"Girls, I had a wonderful summer. Roger met my family, and they love him. We hung out every single weekend." Linda was bubbling over with happiness and hardly let Joann get a word in.

Finally, Joann waved her left hand in front of our faces, and I saw a diamond glittering on her finger. "Joann!" I gasped. "That ring is stunning. When did all this happen?"

"A couple weeks ago," she said, shyly. "We are thinking of getting married in April."

"Not after graduation?" I responded, surprised.

"We just can't wait that long," she said with a laugh.

For the first time, I felt like the odd one out. One day, Joann, for the first time, invited me on a double date with her, Michael, and his new roommate. Joann and I arrived at the restaurant first, and we sat at a table, waiting for our dates. When Michael opened the door, I could not believe my eyes. Right behind him was a blond, blue-eyed giant with a smile that melted my heart. My heart was pounding nearly out of my chest as he approached me, shook my hand, and said, "Hi, I'm David."

Speechless and frozen, I stood gaping at him and holding his hand until Joann nudged me. "I'm Elaine, um, Smith. Elaine Smith," I finally managed to stammer.

"Well, hello, Elaine Smith. Is it really 'Smith,' or is that an alias?" he teased. Then he turned to his roommate. "Michael, why didn't you tell me she was so pretty?"

I knew my cheeks were bright red, and I was so nervous that I remained quiet for most of the date. Knowing the night was nearing its end, I reached for my purse to pay for my part of the tab. David stopped me.

"There is no way you are paying for your meal on our first date!"

Our first date? Was he being serious? I certainly hoped so. I had been waiting for a guy like him my whole life. After David paid, he asked me if he could walk me back to my dorm. I was so nervous that I was afraid I would make a fool of myself, but I agreed. As we headed out of the restaurant, I hid my shaking hands in my pockets and tried to think of something to say.

"So, David, what year are you in?"

"This is my second year."

We were silent again. Then I asked, looking into those blue eyes, "How come you didn't room with Michael last year?"

"I just transferred from another college to be closer to home. And I wanted to take advantage of the free tuition program." He grinned as he looked down at me.

"That's why I came to Bismarck too," I replied.

"Well, maybe we'll get to work together."

"Maybe," I said nervously. "What is your major?"

"Criminal justice."

"No way! That's what I am studying," I said, a

little too eagerly. He was just so likeable. David was the first guy I had ever felt interested in, but it was hard for me to believe that he was truly so interested in me. *He's probably like this with every girl he meets,* whispered a little voice in my head.

"It would be so cool if we ended up working together, Elaine." He reached for my hand. "Have you thought about where you are going to apply after graduation? I know a police force that is hiring."

I pulled my hand away nervously and was glad to see my dorm getting closer. David grabbed my hand again and pulled me around to face him.

"Elaine, do you believe in love at first sight?" he whispered.

"Um, I don't know—I'm not even sure what love feels like." My voice began to shake as I told him how I was left on a doorstep at an orphanage as a newborn.

"So, you don't know your last name or the actual day you were born?" He looked startled. "Elaine, I would be deeply honored if you would take my last name."

I stared at him in shock. "I don't even know you!"

He smiled his big, loveable smile, and to my disbelief, he said, "Elaine Smith, you are going to marry me some day."

"Um, I don't know about that. Good night." I laughed nervously and practically ran back to my room.

Once I was back in my dorm, Joann asked, "What's wrong? Are you okay? I thought David seemed really nice." She stared at me. "You're actually shaking."

"He is nuts." I gasped.

"Why, what did he do? He didn't try anything, did he?" Her eyes blazed angrily.

"No, no, nothing like that," I reassured her. "He asked me if I believed in love at first sight."

"Is that all?" she giggled.

"No, it's not all. He said he was going to marry me, and I don't even know his last name!" I was pacing back and forth in our room.

"Boy, he must have it bad. It's Purdy," laughed Joann.

"Well, I think he's nuts. What's pretty?"

"He is. Not 'pretty,' 'Purdy'. That's his last name. Elaine, sit down. You are still shaking. Are you okay?"

I sat. "My heart is pounding, my hands are sweating, and my stomach feels funny," I replied. "He made me so nervous."

"Sounds like you're in love to me," teased Joann.

"No way." I insisted. "That man is definitely nuts." I flopped down on my bed and let out a long breath.

I spent the whole night tossing and turning. When morning came, I suddenly knew. I sat up and yelled, "I'm in love."

"Go back to sleep," I heard Linda mumble.

"Wait a minute, what did you say?" asked Joann.

Suddenly she was pulling me out of bed and dancing me around the room.

"Elaine is in love. Elaine is in love. I knew you liked him."

"What do I do now? I was rude to him last night. I can't stop thinking about it. I barely got any sleep."

"You have to let him know that you like him." Joann exclaimed.

I shook my head. "I don't think I can do that. I'm so nervous, and I don't want to mess things up. I still don't really believe that he is in love with me. He's so good-looking. What could he possibly see in me?"

Linda piped up. "Elaine, you are so beautiful. Everyone else can see it but you. You have gorgeous hair and perfect skin, and you have the sweetest personality. Also, you have an amazing figure. I'm sure a lot of guys have a crush on you.

There's nothing weird about a good-looking guy falling head over heels in love with you."

The next week was torture. I didn't hear from David at all, and when I asked Joann if David had said anything to Michael, she just shook her head. I was heartbroken. Was David just some psychopath who got a kick out of proposing to every girl he met? Or was he turned off by my lackluster response? Why had I allowed myself to fall in love with a perfect stranger? I pictured his confident, friendly smile and his sincere manner, and I just couldn't believe anything bad about him. There must have been an explanation.

The week dragged on, and finally it was Friday. Around 1 PM, after making a feeble attempt to eat lunch, I sat in my room and pondered what I could possibly do to entertain myself all weekend. Suddenly, Joann burst into the room, panting and gasping. She handed me a note and flopped on the bed. "Here," she wheezed. "I nearly died running here from the cafeteria. I'm not cut out for this. I don't get up at the crack of dawn to run every day like you do. I hope you're happy."

I took the note and froze. "Is this from David?"

"Of course, it's from David—just open it!"

"I don't think I can. What if he never wants to see me again, or is already engaged to someone else?"

"Just open it!"

Just then, Linda walked in and grabbed the note. "I'll open it." Her eyes quickly scanned the letter. She smiled. "Aww, somebody has a really big crush on you, Elaine." She began reading:

Dear Elaine Smith,

I would be honored if you would accompany me to dinner tonight. I have so much to tell you. Please dress up. If you are not interested in me, though, I will understand. Please place a white pillowcase in your window if you will accept this invitation. If I see it there, I will pick you up at 7 PM
—David

I jumped up, grabbed my pillowcase, and dashed over to put it in the window. To my surprise, David was waiting in the parking lot outside, and he started waving and jumping up and down as soon as he saw me. I waved back with a big smile. Linda and Joann tackled me.

"Don't let him see you!" hissed Linda. She grabbed the pillowcase and pulled it over my head. Joann yanked down the blinds.

Surely David had witnessed our crazy shenanigans, but I didn't care. I was so excited—but also so nervous to see David. How would he explain the way he had ignored me all week? Was he going to talk about marriage again?

"What should I do, girls? Should I let him know that I like him, or should I be reserved? I don't want him to think I fall in love with everybody."

"You need to play hard-to-get," stated Linda. "If you really are serious about David, keep him guessing for a while. Boys like to feel like they worked hard to win their girl."

Joann disagreed. "You can't play games like that with David. Michael says that when he decides he wants something, he doesn't change his mind. I think it would be mean to tease him."

I dropped my head in my hands and let out a groan. Giggling, the girls pulled me in for a group hug, and Joann whispered, "Just wait and see how the night goes. You're going to have a wonderful time, and I'm sure whatever you do, David will think you are perfect."

"No matter what happens, you are going to be absolutely gorgeous," Linda announced. "When David sees you, he won't know what hit him. It's time for "Operation Bombshell." We will make sure David is groveling at your feet. "Elaine would look absolutely stunning in that emerald-green dress I just bought," Joann said. "What do you think? It's a little small for me, but it would be perfect for her."

The girls seemed so excited to dress me up that I kept my skepticism to myself. I had never spent much time on such unimportant things as makeup, jewelry, and fancy hairstyles. Truth be told, I was a bit of a tomboy, and I was sure that their efforts were going to be wasted. After I washed my hair, Joann helped me to set it in big rollers.

"You need to leave these in all day if you want really glamorous waves."

"All day?" I moaned. "I can't go out like this. How will I do my schoolwork? How can I go to the library wearing these?" Joann yanked open a drawer and pulled out a large, colorful scarf. "Just wear this over your head when you need to go out, and nobody will know. It's worth a little suffering to be beautiful," she joked.

That evening, Joann took out the curlers. My hair fell in shining waves, and with a few well-placed pins, she had me looking so glamorous I barely recognized myself. Then she clasped her genuine pearl necklace around my neck and handed me a pair of lace gloves.

I smiled at my reflection in the mirror and struck a movie-star pose. Who was this girl looking back at me?

Linda stared at me with narrowed eyes for a minute. "Who do you remind me of? I know—you look exactly like Audrey Hepburn from *Roman Holiday.*"

"Yes, yes." Joann chimed in. "I never noticed it before."

My bravado disappeared as soon as I stepped out the door. Waiting in the downstairs hall, I did my best to control my shaking knees and sweaty palms. When the doorbell rang, I thought my heart would pound through my chest.

I hesitated for a moment and then opened the door, and there was the man of my dreams, smiling on the other side. He stood without speaking for what seemed like an eternity.

"Hello, David. Is everything all right?" I asked nervously.

"You are just so beautiful, Elaine." He took a step toward me and grabbed my hand, but I pulled back and looked him in the eyes.

"David, why didn't you at least call me this week?"

"I'm sorry, Elaine. I didn't mean to make you worry. I'll explain everything over dinner."

"Can you please just explain now?"

"Please, Elaine. Just wait until dinner, and I promise you will understand everything."

He walked me to his car, and my mouth fell wide open. Like a gentleman, he opened the door of a shiny Mercedes-Benz. I sat down on the leather seat and stared at the dashboard loaded with fancy gadgets.

"David, whose car is this?"

"It's mine. My parents gave it to me as a graduation present."

"Are you rich?" I blurted out, then reddened as I realized how rude my question must have sounded. However, David didn't seem bothered at all.

"No, my parents own a Mercedes-Benz dealership in Bismarck. They didn't exactly give it to me for free. My parents told me that if I helped them out in the dealership throughout high school, I would receive a car of my choice and weekly spending money."

"That is wonderful." I said. "It was very wise of your parents to have you work for the car instead of just giving it to you."

"My parents are wonderful. You will love them." Now I was nervous. My thoughts raced. *What on earth does he mean? Am I meeting his parents tonight? I am not prepared for this.* Thankfully, my anxious brain was quickly distracted by David's story.

"My parents never handed me anything for free once I was old enough to work," David said. "Of course, they still paid for my food and most other necessities, but I bought all my own clothes, and I learned to save money for things I really wanted.

I still have the first car I bought: a 1953 Chevy Corvette with a blue flame 235 V6 engine, 159 horsepower, and a 2-speed powertrain, automatic transmission that cost me $3,490 new. You are going to love the color. Its red interior, and red and white exterior is beautiful."

"David." I laughed. "All those numbers mean nothing to me. I don't know anything about cars, and I don't even know how to drive." The truth was, though, that I had always been fascinated by automobiles, but growing up in an orphanage, I had not had any opportunities to indulge this interest. I had rarely even been in a car. I tried not to let David see how much I was drooling over his stylish vehicle.

"You need to learn to drive so you can get a license before you join the police force. I have an idea. How about if I give you lessons?" David offered excitedly.

Of course, I took him up on the offer. We finally reached the restaurant, which was inside a country club. David jumped out and opened my door. I noticed he gave the valet attendant his keys and $3.00. I never did like stingy people, and his generosity was certainly a point in his favor. I gave him a quick smile. As we entered the restaurant, my jaw dropped. I stared in wonder at marble floors and columns, a beautiful winding staircase, and a large, sparkling crystal chandelier hanging in the center of the foyer. We were immediately escorted to a lovely dining room with bouquets of different-colored roses on each table. The place was crowded, and there didn't seem to be any empty tables. To my surprise, we were directed to a small room around the corner. Our table had red roses and was surrounded by floor-to-ceiling glass on three sides overlooking a lake. David pulled out a chair for me. I pinched myself to see if I was dreaming. I was in a fairytale, and I felt like the princess.

"Thank you, David. This place is fantastic."

David smiled from ear to ear. "I'm glad you like it. I don't want you to ever forget our first real date."

"So, you are assuming there will be more?" I teased, trying to hide my shaking hands in my lap.

"Elaine, that is up to you." David was squeezing his hands together and twisting his watchband. Suddenly, I realized that he was just as nervous as I was; oddly enough, that made me feel slightly better.

"Let's see how the first one goes," I joked, then immediately hoped he wasn't offended. He just grinned as usual and looked at the menu.

The food was excellent, and while we ate, I asked David to tell me about himself.

"Well, I was very quiet and shy when I was younger."

"I find that hard to believe."

"I only had a small circle of friends, and I was very close with my mom and dad. I was also really into my studies, and I played a lot of basketball. In my spare time I was always tinkering with cars," David went on.

"You certainly don't seem shy now." I remarked.

"When I began working at the auto dealership, I learned how to talk to people, and I became much more confident. I have something to tell you, though, that I think will surprise you." He leaned forward across the table.

"What's that?"

"I've never had a girlfriend. In fact, I've never been on a real date until now," he confided.

"Really, David? You're right—I am surprised. Didn't you know any girls growing up?"

"Yes, I did know a few nice girls, but they were never anything more than friends to me. I never felt anything like the way I felt when I first saw you."

"I've never had a boyfriend either. There weren't many opportunities to meet boys at the orphanage, and although I went on a few dates at college last year, none of them were ever more than just friends," I told him.

"What about me? Am I just a friend, or is there a chance for me?" He looked deeply into my eyes.

I looked down at my lap. Should I tease him again, or tell him the truth? "I guess I do kind of like you, David," I said, unable to stop a huge grin from spreading over my face. "Are you going to tell me why you ignored me all last week?"

"Well, I felt like I completely overwhelmed you last week, and I wasn't sure how you felt about me. I called my mom, and she suggested that I leave you alone for a while to give you a chance to sort out your feelings. My mother knows me so well. She said that I had probably rushed into things too fast and that I might have scared you," he admitted.

"To be honest, you really did intimidate me at first, but as the week went on, I began to realize how much I had enjoyed being with you. It drove me crazy that you never called me. By the end of the week, it was all I could think about."

"I'm sorry, Elaine. I didn't mean to upset you." His smiling face did not back up his words.

"You don't look very sorry, David," I teased.

"I may not have called you, Elaine, but I thought about you all week."

The meal was finished, and our desserts arrived. After we were done, David asked me if I had enjoyed our evening.

"It was magical, David. Thank you so much."

Then David did something I would have never

expected. He moved his chair close to mine, grabbed my hands, and looked deep into my eyes. "Elaine Smith, I think you know I fell in love with you the first time I met you. The hardest thing I ever experienced was not seeing and speaking with you this past week. I know this might seem sudden, but I need to know how you feel about me."

"David Purdy, the truth is that I could hardly sleep thinking about you that night. When I woke up in the morning, I sat up in bed and yelled, 'I'm in love!' "

At that moment, David grabbed me and kissed me. I had never been kissed before, or been shown any type of physical affection, for that matter. The nuns at the orphanage had been very kind, but they were certainly not affectionate. It felt so natural, and absolutely amazing. I wondered if anyone was watching, and then I realized that I didn't care. David got down on one knee and opened a small box with a diamond ring in it. "Elaine, I cannot hold back my feelings for you, and I pray that you feel the same. I want to spend the rest of our lives as husband and wife."

I was so overwhelmed with emotions that I could not speak; all I could do was nod my head yes, as he placed this beautiful ring on my finger. Before I could even get a good look at it he kissed me again. From the other room I heard cheering. A tall, handsome man with a little grey at his temples and an elegant woman rushed into the room and enveloped both of us in a bear hug.

"Elaine, this is my mother, Louise, and my father, Jake," David grinned.

"It's so nice to meet you, Mr. and Mrs. Purdy," I said shyly.

"Oh, Elaine," gushed Mrs. Purdy, "You are just as beautiful as David said you were. We've been praying for David to meet someone just like you for so long. Welcome to our family, dear."

Mr. Purdy gave me a kiss on the cheek and said, "I hope we aren't overwhelming you. David said you are shy. We are just so excited."

"Mr. and Mrs. Purdy, I have never had a family before, so I am not used to all this, but I think it is absolutely wonderful."

I asked his parents if they felt we were going a little too fast. They both laughed, and Louise proceeded to tell me their story.

"Elaine, Jake and I were married thirty days after we met. We knew from our first encounter that we would be married. We have always told David that when you meet the right one, you'll know. David has impeccable taste, and we trust his judgment completely. I know that he would never make such a big decision without a lot of prayer."

I gulped. "I hope we are not getting married in one month."

Louise patted my arm reassuringly. "Of course not, Elaine. The timing is between you, David, and God, but we will support whatever you decide. I'm a strong believer in short engagements. I know this is all very sudden for you though, so take your time."

"But we do want to get married soon," David interjected. "Not in a month, of course, but how about at the end of the school year?"

I thought about this and then nodded.

"Yes, I think that is a good idea. That will give us enough time to get to know each other better and complete our studies without too many distractions."

"We will definitely get to know each other better, but I don't agree with you about the distractions," teased David. "If you aren't a distraction, I don't know what is."

"It's really important that you both keep up with your studies," responded Mr. Purdy. "As exciting as this all is, you will be very young when you get married, and you will need good paying jobs to be able to keep house. I know David has some savings, but you will be surprised how fast the money goes once you have bills to pay. So, my advice is to buckle down on your work and don't let your relationship cause your grades to slide."

Mrs. Purdy nodded in agreement. "You need to save as much as possible in the beginning before you have children and have to stay home. Once the babies come, it is so much harder to save money."

Babies?! I thought to myself. As strange as it seems, I had never thought about this possibility. Growing up in an orphanage does not give one warm and rosy feelings about childhood and family life. I knew absolutely nothing about being a parent. I felt a momentary stab of panic.

The school year went by quickly, and our wedding day was inching closer. David's mother asked my permission to make all the arrangements, and I agreed, with only one stipulation: I wanted the wedding to be simple. I was uncomfortable with a lot of fuss and a lot of strangers staring at me. Mrs. Purdy was very sympathetic and understanding, and I found myself thinking more and more of my birth mother. Somehow, I imagined her to be something like Louise. In fact, I began to fantasize that they were best friends, and I imagined Louise and my mother with their heads together, sipping tea and making plans for the wedding.

One Saturday, Louise showed up on campus. "Are you busy today, Elaine? We need to do some shopping."

"Well, I really need to work on my research paper today. It's due next week, and I still have quite a bit left to do."

"You can work on it later, although don't tell Jake I'm distracting you from your schoolwork. Men never think that clothes are important."

"Thanks so much for inviting me, Louise, but I really am very busy."

"The wedding will be here before you know it, and you still haven't picked out a dress." Louise exclaimed.

I sighed. It was time to stop procrastinating and tell her the real reason I couldn't go shopping.

"Louise, I don't have enough money to buy a dress. I was just going to borrow a dress from one of my roommates. After all, we don't want a big ceremony, and the dress really isn't that important. Besides, David and I want to stand on our own two feet and be responsible. If we start letting you pay for things now, we'll set a bad precedent."

"Elaine, you would be doing me a big favor if you let me buy you a dress. Jake and I were engaged and married so quickly that I was never able to purchase a special gown, and I couldn't have afforded one anyway. I don't regret a thing; Jake is the most wonderful husband any woman could ever ask for. I can't help dreaming sometimes, though, about what it would have been like to be married in a beautiful white wedding dress. If you would let me buy you a dress, you would make me very happy." Louise smiled at me and patted my hand.

Tender Answers the Call

How could I say no? My dream dress had a fitted satin bodice trimmed with handmade lace and a full skirt covered in layers of tulle. A matching tulle veil cascaded from a simple tiara nearly to my waist. I still don't know how much it cost; Mrs. Purdy refused to let me ask the price or look at the tag.

That night, the Purdys invited me over for dinner. Although I knew David had a younger sister we had never met. Mary was fifteen years old, and she was adorable with her blonde bob. Like David, she was tall and had a huge smile and lots of dimples. After dinner, she asked me to try on my dress. It would have to be returned to the shop for some minor alterations in a couple of weeks, but for now it hung in Mary's closet, looking like a misty cloud that had accidentally fallen from the sky and landed in a teenager's bedroom.

"May I try it on?" she asked shyly. Of course, I agreed. I hoped this was the first step to becoming fast friends. She was so exactly like the little sister I wished I had.

"So, how does someone manage to get engaged in a week?" she asked curiously, changing back into her own clothes.

I told her all about that first week with David.

"You are just perfect for my brother," she remarked.

"Why do you say that?" I asked.

"Well, one day we were having a serious conversation about the type of person we wanted to marry someday, and he described you to a T."

Just then, we heard David's footsteps in the hall.

"Quick, shut the closet door. It's bad luck for a groom to see the dress before the wedding. Promise me you'll guard your closet with your life." I whispered frantically.

"What are you two whispering about?" David asked suspiciously, coming into the room. "Mary, what are you telling her? You'd better not be messing things up for me."

"Oh, I was about to tell her about what you did to my diary when I was eight . . . and the time you broke the window, and we told mom that it was—" Mary teased.

"Okay, okay! What do you want from me?" David threw up his hands in surrender.

"I promise not to tell her any more stories if you promise to let me hang out with my new sister on campus now and then."

"Of course, you can hang out with me, Mary." I said quickly. "Any time you have your parents' permission, you are welcome to come and spend the weekend with me and my roommates. I know they would just love you." Over the next several months

Mary slept over every Saturday night. I was amazed at how much fun we girls had talking and laughing about the men in our lives, and Mary seemed to have a new boy chasing her every few weeks.

Our wedding date was May 25, 1957, the day after graduation. When the day finally arrived, I was a mess. The year had gone by so quickly, and everything suddenly seemed unreal, like a story that I had heard about someone else.

"It's not too late to change your mind, girl," teased Linda. "I have a getaway car parked right outside."

For a moment, I considered her offer. Then I came to my senses. David was the man God had chosen to be my husband. Everything I had learned about him as the year went on had confirmed this. For better or for worse, this was the path I was meant to take.

Linda, Joann, and Mary were helping me dress in the Purdy's' master suite. David and his groomsmen had stayed in the lower level of the home. We all jumped when we heard a knock on the door.

"Come in—unless you're David." called Linda.

Mrs. Purdy cracked the door and poked her head through. "How is everything going in here? David and his groomsmen left early. You still have a few minutes if you're not quite done. Although I can't imagine what you would need to do to look any more beautiful, Elaine. You are going to be the loveliest bride ever to walk down the aisle of our church."

"Thank you, Mrs. Purdy," I said shyly.

"Young ladies, why don't you head downstairs for a minute so I can talk to my new daughter alone." Louise shooed the other girls out the door.

As soon as the door closed behind my friends, Louise took my hands in hers.

"Elaine, I know it might be hard for you at first, but I would be so honored if you would call me 'Mom' and think of me as your mother. I know it might seem awkward to you, since you've never had a mother, but if you could just think about it and get used to the idea, Jake and I would be so happy. Jake feels the same way."

I was glowing with happiness as I walked down the stairs with my new mother, climbed into a white limousine, and headed to the church, where my life would be changed forever.

TWO

The Wedding

As we approached the church, the girls were quiet, understanding that I was much too nervous for small talk. When we all exited the limousine, we saw David's dad, who was going to walk me down the aisle, standing at the top of the church stairs. With hushed voices, everyone figured out where they were supposed to be. An usher appeared at Mrs. Purdy's elbow and escorted her to her seat.

The familiar notes of Pachelbel's Canon began to play. The groomsmen, handsome in black tuxedos, lined up next to the girls, who wore long, yellow chiffon gowns. David's cousins were to escort Joann and Linda, and a childhood friend Michael Wood, the best man, stood next to Mary, who was the maid of honor. They slowly glided down the aisle, two by two. Meanwhile, Mr. Purdy and I were the last two out in the church foyer. "Kind of reminds me of the animals entering the ark," he muttered out of the side of his mouth. I giggled. It was such a silly remark, but I suddenly felt much more relaxed. I waited for my signal.

The notes of Pachelbel's Canon died away, and the organist began playing the Wedding March. "That's our cue," smiled Mr. Purdy.

"Mr. Purdy, thanks for accepting me into your family. You are the best mom and dad I could ask for."

"Elaine, we prayed for you for many years before we actually met. Your heavenly Father has been watching over you, and He is the one who brought you to us."

As we stepped through the doors, I saw David waiting for me at the front of the church. The long walk down the aisle seemed like an eternity, and I was tempted to break into a run.

When we reached the front, Pastor Bob asked, "Who gives this woman to be wed to this man?"

Mr. Purdy answered, "Her future mother and father."

Next, Pastor Bob told us to hold hands. As we did, I noticed that David's hands were shaking. I smiled reassuringly at him, forgetting that he couldn't see my face through the long veil.

Pastor Bob instructed the congregation to sit. "Did you ever hear the story of the black veil?" I shot a horrified glance at David, who looked slightly frozen. Pastor Bob never could resist the temptation to tell a corny story or joke.

The pastor continued, "This young man wanted to marry someone's daughter, but she wore a black veil, so the groom never saw his bride's face. It was nighttime, and after the simple ceremony, they went right to their quarters and fell asleep. When morning came, the young man discovered that it wasn't the girl he loved. It was her sister. "So, David, do you want to check under that veil?" David looked startled, lifted the veil and gave a thumbs up, but then he looked at Pastor Bob and said, "she doesn't even have a sister." Mary started giggling as the congregation started to laugh.

"If you are interested in knowing what happened to the man who married the wrong sister, read Genesis 29." Pastor Bob paused a moment, then continued: "Dearly beloved, we are gathered here today to unite David Purdy and Elaine Smith in holy matrimony." David squeezed my hand. "They will now share their vows with each other." I took a deep breath. "David, I never thought I would fall in love, never mind at first sight. I didn't know what love was, since I never had parents or grandparents, siblings, aunts, or uncles to say they loved me. After seeing how your family loves one another, I have hope, because I love every one of them. Thank you, because soon I will have a family, I can call my own." I heard a couple of guests sniffling. "I will say that you intimidated me on our first encounter. You were so confident." Looking at the crowd, I added, "I only knew David for a few hours, and I didn't even know his last name when he said that he was going to marry me. At first, I thought he was crazy, but he wasn't." A few guests clapped. Then I looked into David's eyes and said, "You were right. Here we are, and I love you so much."

David began, "Elaine, I have never felt about anyone the way I feel about you. I never understood what people meant by love until I saw you. I love your smile. I love your tender heart. I love your spirit. I've been waiting for a certain girl all my life, and as soon as I saw you, I knew that girl was you."

Pastor Bob asked for the rings. Michael was smiling as he handed the rings to Pastor Bob. "These rings represent the start of a new chapter in a couple's life." As we each placed the rings on one anther's finger, Pastor Bob asked David first. "Do you, David, promise to love, honor, and cherish Elaine, in sickness and in health, till death do you part, so help you God?"

"I do."

"Do you, Elaine, promise to love, honor, and cherish David, in sickness and in health, till death do you part, so help you God?"

"I do."

"By the power vested in me by the state of North Dakota, I now pronounce you husband and wife. David, you may now kiss the bride. Ladies and gentlemen, for the first time in public, I give you Mr. and Mrs. David Purdy."

The reception was held at the Bismarck Country Club. I don't remember much about it because I felt like I was in a dream. As the party wound down, I discovered that David had booked the bridal suite at a hotel nearby. The next morning, we flew to Hawaii for a one-week honeymoon. We toured pineapple plantations and tropical gardens and tried surfing. I thought about the lonely little orphan girl who had never left North Dakota. Was that girl really me?

Before we knew it, we were back in our first apartment as husband and wife. It was in the basement of the home of our Uncle Frank Purdy, the older brother of David's father. He also just happened to be the chief of police.

THREE

Duty Calls

After we returned from Hawaii, we went to the police station to fill out applications for the North Dakota Police Academy. Uncle Frank oversaw selecting twenty-five candidates from our city, from which twelve would be selected to join the force. Most graduates would end up working for the city that sent them, at least at first. Whenever the highly coveted state police positions opened, Academy graduates would be promoted into these jobs. The lady taking my application let me know that no woman from Bismarck had ever completed the training course, and been given a post. I told her I would be the first.

"I like your attitude, and I'll be rooting for you," she said with a wink. "Also, you need to complete the written test as soon as possible. The city is allowing all the recruits to train at the police gym over the summer, and there will be a trainer working with you starting next week—if your application is accepted. Good luck."

"We took the written test the very next day, and by the weekend we had our results.

Uncle Frank sat us down for a serious talk. "Elaine, are you really determined to attend the academy? No woman from Bismarck has ever completed the course, and only a few state-wide have gone on to become officers. It is the toughest in the country. If you are to have any chance of passing, you are going to have to work twice as hard as the men. You are also going to have to deal with some harassment and teasing. Many of the men you are training with are going to be uncomfortable with your presence, and they will give you a hard time, especially if you perform better than they do."

"And I bet she will." interrupted David.

"A lot of men don't like to be shown up by women. It's childish, but that's how it is. You are going to need to develop a thick skin," Uncle Frank said.

"Uncle Frank, I'm not expecting it to be easy, but I know I can do it. For as long as I can remember, I have wanted to be on the police force. Besides, this is 1957. There are many women police officers," I said stubbornly.

When I was a little girl, I wrote a school report on Alice Stebbins Wells. Back in 1910, she became the first woman police officer who had the authority to make arrests. I imagined myself as a pioneer like Alice, forging new trails in the police force for women and expanding their roles.

"Uncle Frank, Elaine is much stronger than she looks, and she can run circles around me. I believe in her," David said earnestly.

What David said was true. My love of running had often landed me in trouble at the orphanage, but in college I took advantage of the running track available to all students. By the time I graduated, I could run a mile in under six minutes.

"I believe in both of you, for that matter. Your grades from the criminal justice program are exceptional, and you both have a very strong work ethic. I put myself out on a limb when I nominated you two, but the committee was very impressed by your applications, and you are among the twenty-five recruits," Uncle Frank said, smiling.

"Thank you so much for letting us know, Uncle Frank, and for all you've done for us. I promise you that we'll make you proud." David grabbed my hand and squeezed it.

"While you are waiting to be sent to the academy, you will be training at the police gym. I recommend you head over there now to talk to the trainer. I think he is an old friend of yours, David. He has quite a workout schedule planned for the recruits. Oh, and one more thing. When you see me at the station, address me as 'Chief Purdy,' not 'Uncle Frank.' And David, when you are at work, you and Elaine are police officers, not husband and wife. Do you understand what I mean?"

"I think so, Uncle Frank—I mean, Chief Purdy. It'll be difficult, though."

"We are making an exception by allowing the two of you to train together. David, I know this will be hard, but if there is an issue between Elaine and another employee, you cannot get involved."

Later that day, David and I headed to the training room to sign in. There I met Kevin Dunne, a friend of David's. I had always considered David to be one of the most fit men I knew, but Kevin looked like Mr. Universe. David and Kevin shook hands. "Kevin, so good to see you. I would like to introduce you to my wife, Elaine. Elaine, Kevin, and I go way back."

"Davey, no way a beautiful girl like this would marry a hillbilly like you." teased Kevin. Suddenly he lunged at David, and the two of them were locked in what looked like a struggle to the death. David turned bright red, and beads of sweat broke out on his forehead. I was trying to figure out if I should rescue him when they broke apart and started laughing.

"I can still kick your butt, but I don't want to kill you in front of your lovely wife," laughed Kevin.

"You and what army?" For a moment I thought they were going to start wrestling again.

"Are you children finished?" I interjected.

"Yes," David responded and started to explain. "We've been doing this since we were about six years old. Kevin never wins."

"Elaine," Kevin pleaded, "please believe me, Davey cheats. It's the only way the poor guy can win. I feel kind of bad for him."

With a smile, I responded, "I believe you. David hates to lose."

"I like this girl." said Kevin, grinning.

"She has good taste in husbands," David bragged.

"Let's get down to business. Davey, are you signing up for the police training?"

"Did you mean, are *we* signing up for the police training?" I asked.

Kevin's mouth dropped open. "A pretty girl like you?"

"Yes, I plan on being the first woman in Bismarck to graduate from the State Police Academy."

Kevin let out a low whistle. "It's a tough test, and you must meet the same requirements as the men. I'll do my best to help you get ready, but I've never trained a woman before. Frankly, I'm not sure if you can do what I'm going to ask from you. I will say that the guys are going to enjoy training with someone so decorative. The place looks better already."

I rolled my eyes. No matter what I had to do, I was going to prove that I wasn't just a decoration.

Kevin pulled out a clipboard. "Okay, let's get started. We have a rigorous training program. Starting Monday through Friday, you will report here at 7 AM to run on the track. I recommend two days working on sprinting and three days working on distance running. By the end of the training, everyone should be able to run a half marathon."

He looked at me. "That's 13.1 miles."

"Yes, I know. I did quite a lot of running in college. I usually did a long run of 10 to 12 miles at least once a week."

"Oh!" He paused for a second, looking surprised. "We are also going to be doing calisthenics and weightlifting for an hour a day. David can spot you when you are lifting, Elaine. I'll have to check and see if we have some dumbbells that would work for you." He paused. "We also have a brand-new obstacle course. You're going to really like it, Davey."

We headed out. "Take me home, Davey," I teased. "I need to get some rest before Monday."

Monday came, and I noticed only twenty-three candidates had reported. Kevin led the run, along with one of the police officers. "Gentlemen and ... lady," he announced. A few candidates whistled and stared in my direction. "This is Officer Louis Matterson, and he is going to time you on the track today. Just do your best; we have twelve weeks to improve."

When the starting gun went off, I broke into an easy stride. For the first mile, we all ran in a pack, but as we began the second mile on the quarter-mile track, I could see some of the guys were becoming winded. I began passing the others, one by one. Clearly, these guys did not run every day like I did. Soon, I was right behind David. One of the men stumbled to the side of the track, and I heard him losing his breakfast.

After we finished, we walked over to Officer Matterson to look at our times. The guy who had gotten sick aimed a dirty look at me. David glared back. I nudged him in the ribs, and his scowl changed to a smile.

During calisthenics, Kevin gave me the option of doing push-ups on my knees, but I bravely battled through fifty push-ups on my toes. If the boys could do it, so could I. Pull-ups didn't go quite as well. I could only do three, and all the men did at least ten. Weightlifting was even worse. I was lifting half of what the other candidates were, and not all of them were in good shape. We rode home in silence, sweaty and exhausted.

Finally, I spoke up. "David, if I don't improve, I will not make it. After two years of studying criminal justice, I have not come this far not to give it my best."

"I thought you did great, Elaine. You outran most of the men."

By week two, however, some of the men were starting to keep up with me on the track, but I was only up to five pull-ups.

On Saturday, I quietly crawled out of bed at 6 AM and tied on my sneakers. As I tiptoed to the door, I heard a noise.

"Hold on, Elaine. We're partners, remember? I'm going with you." We ran for an hour, then stopped at a café for breakfast. "Elaine, I talked to Kevin yesterday. He is really impressed with you, and he wants both of us to succeed. He gave us special permission to go back to the gym in the afternoon and do some extra workouts. You must be exhausted; would you even want to do that?"

"Yes. You are a mind reader, honey. I don't

know how I'll ever keep up if I don't try harder than everyone else. I've been thinking about it all week. I know I can do this if I just work harder. That is so kind of Kevin."

"Kevin would do anything for me—we're like brothers, and I helped him get out of a couple of tight jams when we were kids. Letting us use the gym is no big deal—but I'll tell him you said thanks. He asked me if you had a sister," teased David.

On the following Monday, we began training in martial arts. I was a little nervous, but I was confident that I could keep pace with the men. I had a secret that nobody else knew, not even David. When it was finally my turn, I was paired with the largest candidate. He sniggered and rolled his eyes. Then he lifted his hands to the instructor as if to say, "Really?"

"Listen," the instructor said, "you are all going to face men or women bigger or smaller than you, and you will need to be able to take him or her down. So, Adam, you won't do Elaine any favors if you go easy on her. Understand?"

"Yes, sir."

"Don't worry, I'll go easy on you," I boasted.

"Okay, princess."

Everyone started to laugh. The instructor

explained what to do, and I approached my opponent. Smirking, he reached out to grab me by the arm, and found himself flat on his back. He jumped up, his face bright red. He put up his fist and took a swing at my face. I ducked under, punched him in the side, grabbed his arm, twisted it back, and put him on the floor again.

"Little lady," said the instructor. "You're no princess. You're the fastest learner I've ever had." His eyes scanned the recruits. "Who else wants to try laying a hand on 'Wonder Woman'?" A few confident hands shot up.

One by one, I tossed every single member of the class. They all looked at me with new respect. I tried to be gentle with David, but not so with the others. It wouldn't hurt them to learn a lesson.

"As you can see, gentlemen, self-defense is all about technique. Not only is size and strength unimportant, but your opponent can use it against you. The bigger you are, the harder you fall. Give our little superhero a hand," the instructor said to the class.

Everyone smiled and clapped.

We headed home. "Elaine, you never cease to amaze me. How did you do that? We had the same instructions you did, but you blew everyone else away."

"I have a little secret," I confessed. "This isn't my first time using martial arts."

"Really? Where does a girl like you pick up martial arts skills?"

"Well, when I was quite young, a man came to the orphanage and offered to teach all the girls. A patron of the orphanage agreed to pay the man's salary, and the nuns decided that self-defense would be a good addition to our classes."

"So how long did you take lessons?"

"Twelve years."

David gave a low whistle. "You are a dangerous girl. Thank goodness you've never been really mad at me. I will have to watch my step."

"Well, it was a lot more useful than some of the things we learned, like playing the accordion."

"The *accordion?*" David made a face.

"Don't knock it. It's all in the technique, just like martial arts. My accordion playing is lovely. I'm good at playing polkas."

"I'll take your word for it," he said with a grimace.

By the end of the summer, I was one of the fastest distance runners, and fifth best on the obstacle course. I was second worst in the class for weight training, but nobody could ever beat me in martial arts. We were reminded that only twelve spots were open at the academy, but those who weren't chosen could reapply the following year. David and I both ended up being chosen. A few days later, we received a letter of acceptance and a packet from the police academy, which included a letter from the state house.

August 28, 1957
The State House

Welcome, recruits.

Thank you for choosing to serve your state in public service. Let me begin by wishing you all a safe and successful journey. You are about to embark on a difficult course of study and training. You have been selected for your character, knowledge, and abilities, and we are so proud to have you represent North Dakota. May God bless all of you men and women, and may God bless North Dakota.

Best wishes,
Governor John E. Davis

We reported to the academy the following Monday and attended an orientation. The speaker explained that one of the men's dorms was reconstructed to accommodate the women recruits. David and I would only see one another at meals and training. Recruits were not allowed to fraternize, although in the weeks to follow I discovered that many recruits broke this rule and met up in town. How was I going to get through sixteen weeks without David? My mind wandered as I recalled some of the wonderful memories of the past months.

The speaker began explaining about demerits. It was a lot like college, although a little stricter. Being late to anything was an automatic demerit. Rumpled uniforms, unmade beds, and failure to keep dorms tidy to the satisfaction of the room inspectors could all be causes of demerits. Receiving one hundred demerits, engaging in any action of violence, or being unable to complete the training were all grounds for automatic dismissal.

Our dorms were functional but not homey or comfortable. There were ten women recruits, and only one other one was married. She and I hung out when the others went out for a night on the town. We didn't have much in common with the others; most of their conversations were about which male recruits they thought were cute and who they were going to date just as soon as they graduated. My new friend, Doris, cried the first couple of nights, but soon we were too busy to think about missing our husbands. Doris never graduated; a month before we finished, she discovered that she was pregnant. Even though her dream of being a policewoman had to go on the back burner, she seemed happy, and I was envious of her.

The sixteen weeks passed much more quickly than I ever expected. Some of the courses, such as forensic science, were very familiar to me, but I had never handled a gun before, and I had to work hard at target practice. I was still an inexperienced driver, so the driving course was also a challenge.

One hundred and nineteen recruits graduated, including David and me. Four other women also graduated, and so, although I was one of the first women to graduate from the academy, I wasn't the only one. I felt so proud to be in a group of such talented women. At the graduation and awards ceremony, David received a plaque for being the top overall recruit in the class of 1957. I received an award for having the highest skill in martial arts, and although my combined overall ranking for all courses was 36 out of 119, I was the top-scoring woman.

Governor John E. Davis and Col. Walter Stoney of the state police officiated the ceremony. We all wore our new city or state uniforms. They fit perfectly, as we were measured before we left for training. David and I both wore city uniforms; he had been offered a state police job but had turned it down so that we could work together. "The time isn't right," he told me. "I may consider it in the future, once we start a family and need the extra income."

The time we had all been waiting for finally came. The governor came forward and asked us all to repeat an oath. He began by saying, "Please raise your right hand."

I do solemnly swear that I will support the Constitution of the United States and the Constitution of the State of North Dakota; that I will bear true allegiance to the same and defend them against enemies, foreign and domestic, and that I will faithfully and impartially discharge the duties of a police officer, to the best of my ability, so help me God.

After the ceremony, everyone threw their hats in the air and yelled. David and I kissed. Then we all headed to the ballroom for a night of food, fun, and relaxation. The following day, we were to report to the Bismarck Police Department.

For the first year, we had the late-night shift from 11 PM to 8 AM. I was partnered with veteran Jack Connolly, who had been on the force for nearly ten years. He taught me a lot. One day, I asked him why he preferred the graveyard shift, and he explained that his wife, Cheryl, had the same shift at the hospital. David's veteran partner was Philip Brown, who had been on the graveyard shift for six years. He was single and liked to spend his afternoons on his boat.

The following year, when the new recruits came in, we were offered an assignment on the day shift. There was not much action on the graveyard shift, and we had never completely adjusted to being up all night and asleep all day, so we jumped at the chance. The day shift did have a lot more activity. Over the three years, we made over 450 arrests and were top in the department. Then David and I became eligible to interview for detective positions, since we met the minimum requirement of three years of experience and 300 arrests. There were eighteen officers trying out for a handful of openings, and all were much older and more experienced than we were. However, we were told that the written exam weighed heavily in the decision, and David and I both were excellent students and always did well on tests.

About six weeks later, we were asked to report to Chief Purdy's office before roll call. When we arrived, we found Sergeant Brule there too. Chief Purdy said that he wanted to let us know that he had nothing to do with the selection of the detectives. He had chosen not to be involved this year due to a conflict of interest. He asked us not to blame him and added, "Don't be upset with Sergeant Brule either. He had to make some hard decisions, and all the candidates were very qualified." He had an odd expression on his face.

David and I both assured them that we were all right with not making it on our first attempt and that we would apply the next time there were openings.

Sergeant Brule, who had been very quiet until now, said, "Thank you so much. That takes a lot of pressure off me, considering this was the first time the decision was up to me. I am very sorry to tell you that Detective David Purdy and Detective Elaine Purdy will report directly to Chief Purdy at 8 AM starting next Monday. Seeing his ugly mug is not the way I'd like to start off my week, but I suppose the two of you will be very happy about this. Congratulations."

We both looked at each other and could not catch our breaths for a moment. "Thank you so much, Sergeant Brule and Chief Purdy!" I exclaimed.

"Yes, thank you so much. I am thrilled to have this new opportunity," David chimed in.

"You know, this interview was the final stage of the test. I wasn't completely sure I would select the two of you until the words came out of my mouth. You both demonstrate strong character, and that is something we value highly in this station. Your humility, respect, and ability to get along well with the other officers is very important to us. I'm sure you will do excellent work."

We went shopping on the way home, as I needed to purchase some work clothes. I had never worn anything but a uniform to work, and now I was expected to have office wear. After shopping, we stopped at a nice restaurant for a dinner celebration. As luck would have it, a fight broke out at the bar. We both looked at each other, and I said, "Let's have some fun." With a sweeping bow, David said, "After you, my dear." I approached the bar and pulled out my badge. One man stopped and threw up his hands, but the other drew a gun. "Do you know what this is, little lady?"

Using a technique, I had taught to every officer at the academy, I removed the weapon with a twisting motion, unfortunately breaking his wrist at the same time. As he screamed in pain, two other officers arrived, having been called in by the management.

While one officer called an ambulance, the other asked us to fill out an incident report.

"Can we do it later? We're having a sort of celebration," David said.

Suddenly the officer recognized us and grinned.

"Of course, Officer Purdy; just fill it out at the station later."

After we finished our meal, the manager thanked us and let us know the meal was on the house. We declined and insisted that we pay the bill in full, as police policy stated that no officer could receive a gift or money in the line of duty. The bill we received still seemed discounted, and the restaurant owner told us to come in for a free meal sometime when we were not on duty.

Then we reported to the station. The sergeant let us know there were outstanding warrants on both men. They were on the most-wanted list for several bank robberies from Texas to Maine. "Good collar, you two!" he exclaimed.

Over the next three years, we were regarded as the top detective team in the department. We had the highest conviction rate, at 80 percent. It was the 20 percent that haunted us the most.

FOUR

Tender Picks Her Parents

As time passed, we were able to move into our first home as a married couple. It was a dream of mine, while in the orphanage to own a ranch house, with a farmer's porch and a garage. My only disappointment was that none of the babies predicted by my mother-in-law had materialized although I kept having reoccurring dreams of a little girl lost in a big crowd. David believed I might be pregnant. I told him I was not sure. Meanwhile, our friends and relatives were all busy with growing families. One Saturday in July, I attended a party celebrating the fourth birthday of David's cousin Alex's little girl. Alex was Chief Purdy's son. David had to head to the office to finish up some reports, so I went shopping alone. I loved buying gifts for children, perhaps because I had not had many toys myself as a child. I had purchased Raggedy Anne and Andy dolls for the birthday girl. As I struggled to get the big package out of the trunk, a taxi pulled up in front of the house, and a little girl climbed out. The driver waved me over and handed me a box. "For you, miss," he said with a smile. The little girl grabbed my free hand and grinned. "I love parties, don't you?" she confided. "I bet you'd like to know what's in the box. Can we play twenty questions? You make guesses, and I'll say yes or no."

She kept up a steady flow of chatter all the way into the house. Alex's wife, Loriann, came over and hugged me after taking the boxes to the gift table. "Elaine, this is a surprise. How nice of you to bring a guest to play with Anne. She will be thrilled. Whose little girl is this?" I started to explain, but Loriann had already turned away to greet another guest, and the little girl had made a beeline for Anne. How strange it was that Loriann did not recognize the child. No doubt she was a child from Anne's school, and the mother would be by to collect her later.

More children began arriving, and I forgot about the little girl. David finally stopped by, and we sat on the back deck with Alex, eating hot dogs and hamburgers and enjoying the sunny weather. Loriann and Mary were inside entertaining the children. After a while, David looked at his watch and stood up.

"I'm sorry, Alex, but Elaine and I need to run. We must attend a retirement ceremony, and we need to head home and change first."

Police Sergeant Philip Saint-Pierre was retiring after thirty years of service, and it was a mandatory event. Every police officer was in attendance, except for a few of the newer officers whose job it was to make sure that the criminals weren't allowed to overrun the city while the police force partied. To be fair, our parties never got out of hand. Chief Purdy was a firm teetotaler and always kept the bar closed at our official functions. Some of the officers grumbled, but he was adamant. Before he took over, there had been a function at which fighting had broken out, and it had been a huge embarrassment for the force. The closed bar was a big improvement.

As David and I sat nibbling on hors d'oeuvres, I was suddenly paged to the front desk for a phone call. It was Loriann, and she sounded panicked.

"Elaine, did you forget something? Something very important?"

"What do you mean, Loriann?" I asked, bewildered.

"The little girl. you brought! She's still here. Was somebody supposed to pick her up?"

"Loriann, I didn't bring her. I've never seen her before in my life. I met her walking into your house, and I assumed that she was one of Anne's friends from school. Do you mean her mother never picked her up?"

"My goodness, Elaine, who is she? What do I do? Should I talk to Chief Purdy?"

"No, he's having a nice time, and I don't want to bother him. David and I will come pick up the little girl."

I explained the situation to David, and we hurried back to their house. When we arrived, Alex brought us upstairs, where Loriann was sitting on the edge of their bed, questioning the child.

"Loriann, have you asked her who she is?"

"Oh yes," replied Loriann, nodding her head, "and you are not going to believe her answer!"

The child smiled mischievously. She really was a cute girl, with two shining brown pigtails that stuck straight out from her head, and lots of freckles. From the time we walked into the room, she had a grin that went from ear to ear as she gazed at David and me. Loriann said that was the first time that she had smiled.

Using my strict, you-better-tell-me-the-truth voice, I asked, "Young lady, what is your name?"

Still smiling, she said, "Tender Purdy."

Tender Answers the Call

I gasped and covered my mouth. David just looked at me, his eyebrows raised.

Loriann continued, "Wait till you hear this. Tender, who are your mother and father?"

The child pointed to David and me, and then she said, "My mother is Elaine Purdy, and my father is David Purdy."

"I think I need to sit down. Sweetie, you know that's not true. And how do you know our names? We've never seen each other before today." I put my arm around the tiny shoulders.

"It is true, it is," insisted Tender. Her small face began to crumple, and I realized she was about to cry. "My mommy told me that you were going to be my new parents. She *said* you were."

"Who is your mommy, Tender?"

"She wrote you a letter. It's in the box," said Tender.

Loriann paced the room nervously. "Alex," she asked suddenly, "when did you finish the puzzle?"

"What?" Alex seemed confused. "Oh, that puzzle? Didn't you finish it?"

"How would I have done that? I've been running around the house like mad man today, preparing for the party."

"I did the puzzle. I was hiding in your room, and the butterflies were so pretty. Am I in trouble?" Tender looked up nervously.

"Of course not, Tender," said Loriann soothingly. "You shouldn't tell lies, though. A little girl like you couldn't do a big puzzle like that all by yourself. You're not in trouble, but we know somebody must have helped you. Who else came up here?"

Tender scowled. "I don't tell lies. I'm a good girl, and I'm really smart, I like puzzles. I don't need anybody to help me."

Alex glanced nervously at the angry little face screwed up into what looked like the beginning of a tantrum. "Maybe she did complete the puzzle."

"Seriously, Alex? I only had the outer edge completed. It's a thousand-piece puzzle. It would've taken several hours for you and me to finish it; how could a child have done it?"

I gave her shoulders a gentle squeeze. "Tender, nobody is upset with you. We were just wondering who could have done the puzzle."

"My mommy said I was special. I am very smart. I'll prove it if you don't believe me." Tender sobbed and hiccupped between each word. "I could do a harder puzzle than that."

"I believe you, sweetie. How about if we look at your special box."

As we all headed downstairs, Loriann explained, "Anne opened the box, thinking it was one of her presents, but it contained only papers. We never read them, Elaine, because your name was on the outside, so we thought you left it here by mistake."

The battered cardboard box was sitting on the coffee table. Inside were a couple of sheets of stationery covered in very shaky and spidery writing. Underneath the papers were piles of fat envelopes tied together with string.

"My mommy wrote you a letter," Tender informed me again. I began to read aloud.

Dear Elaine and David,

You don't know who I am, but I know all about you. What I am about to ask you to do will come as a shock. Please read this letter through to the end and consider carefully before you make your decision.

If you are reading this, you have met my Tender, and maybe you have already discovered that she is unusual. Also, if you are reading this, it means I have passed away.

David and I exchanged startled glances.

Like you, Elaine, I was dropped off at an orphanage by someone I did not know. I was about one month old, and all that was in my basket was my first name. The orphanage gave me my last name. Like you, I was hoping some distant relative would come and rescue me from that place; but no one ever came. I sometimes wondered if the person who dropped me off was like me. The orphanage treated me fine, but unlike you, I did not receive a higher education. On my eighteenth birthday, I was given a few dollars and sent on my way. With no training and no knowledge of the world, I was ready to fall victim to anything. I really believed in true love and found a man who I thought cared about me. He introduced me to drugs, and before I knew it, I was a heroin addict. I lost my job and was evicted from my apartment, and my boyfriend abandoned me. With no work and nowhere to live, I made a lot of bad decisions, and for a while I kept company with several different men for a few dollars to support my heroin addiction. One of them gave me the greatest gift I could ever receive, my precious Tender.

After I discovered I was pregnant, I went to a church in the neighborhood that helped women with addictions. It was challenging, but I overcame my addiction to protect my child. The shelter allowed me to stay until my baby was one year old. By then, I had found a job and was given free daycare by the state I was in. It was not North Dakota. All was going well. I was now two years sober, and I wanted to give my child a happy life.

Around this time, I started getting excruciating migraines and was diagnosed with brain cancer. I didn't understand why God would do this to me. Hadn't I already suffered enough? I was trying so hard to be a good role model for my little girl, and I was volunteering several hours a week at the shelter that had helped me. I didn't care so much about myself, but the thought of my little girl being sent to an orphanage was unbearable. Then a miracle happened. No, I wasn't healed, but something happened, and I knew my Tender would be taken care of. I can't tell you the details because I'm sworn to secrecy but suffice to say that I know all about you and David, and I know, Elaine, that you would never want my little girl to grow up in an orphanage the way you and I did.

I looked up from the letter. "David, I'm frightened. How does she know all about me?" I whispered.

David shook his head, mystified. "What else does the letter say?"

I read on.

Tender is not a normal little girl. She taught herself to read at age two, and she read an entire set of encyclopedias. She reads medical journals and mysteries and loves all kinds of puzzles. I believe God has something very special in store for her, and it would be awful to put my amazing little girl in an orphanage. I can't tell you how I know about you or why I've chosen you to be Tender's parents, but I'm begging you to please take care of my special little girl. I know you have no children of your own, and I believe God meant for you to be together as a family.

I've included Tender's birth certificate and letters for you to give her on her birthday every year until she turns twenty-one. Please, don't condemn Tender to the life I had to endure. I know I can trust you.

P.S. Enclosed are all the legal documents for you to sign awarding you guardianship of Tender. Please do not attempt to locate Tender's attorney. On special occasions you may hear from him or her.

There was no signature. I stared at the others in stunned silence.

"I told you," Tender said happily. "My mommy is with Jesus, and you're my new mommy and daddy. She told me all about you. Can I go to your house now?"

FIVE

A Decision to Make

We took Tender home. There was really nothing else to be done. As obviously intelligent as Tender was, every time we attempted to question her about where she lived before, how she had managed to hire a taxi, and how she knew where to find us, she clammed up and refused to speak. We decided the best thing would be to take her home to go to bed and question her on the following day.

Getting a three-year-old to bed was not as easy as I had imagined. When we pulled into the driveway, Tender bounced up and down in her seat, squealing, "I love this house! I love this house!" David opened her door, and she jumped into his arms with a squeal.

Once inside, she jumped down and began racing from room to room. "Which bedroom is mine? Can

I sleep in this bed?" Since I had not planned on coming home with a three-year-old child, nothing was ready for her. I began mentally to make a list of what we would need for Tender.

"David, where is she going to sleep?"

"Can I sleep with you tonight? Please?" Tender begged.

I was certain that one was supposed to be firm with young children and not give in to wheedling and whining. I had always been critical of friends who spoiled their children and allowed them to sleep in their parents' bed.

I pulled a couple spare blankets out of the closet and folded one up to be a pillow. I laid these out for her on the spare bed.

"This will have to do for now," I told her guiltily. "Good night."

"You're supposed to tell me a story now. You don't know much about being a mom, do you?"

I ignored the rude remark and wracked my brains for something suitable.

"How about 'Goldilocks and the Three Bears'?" I suggested.

"I love that story." Tender nodded enthusiastically.

I did my best to tell the story from memory. Then I bid Tender good night.

Before David and I went to bed, we sat down

to talk about the day. My mind went back to when Sister Mary Ellen told me that she loved me, that would be the only time I heard it in 18 years. "David the day I left the orphanage, I promised Sister Mary Ellen I would look for a way to help others like me. I remembered thinking that I wanted to help some little girl. Could this be *that* little girl?"

David reminded me that we had been praying for God to give us a family of our own. Maybe this could be the answer to our prayers: the start of our family.

Hours later, I woke up to discover Tender snuggled up next to me in our bed. I was much too tired to take her back to bed, and I decided that just one night wouldn't make much difference.

Breakfast the next morning was an interesting affair. As I shuffled sleepily to the fridge, wondering what little girls liked to eat, Tender came bouncing out of the bedroom.

"Good morning, new Mommy and Daddy. Don't open the refrigerator. I want to guess what's in it." She climbed up onto a chair and stood looking around the room.

"Tender, get down from there. You'll fall." scolded David.

"Hold on, I need to look around." She continued scanning the room. "Okay, you have half a loaf of bread, a small container of cream for coffee (which is expired), hot dogs, hamburgers, relish, mustard, ketchup, one piece of cake, and one jar of jalapeño peppers. There is also one stick of butter, one jar of grape jam, and six eggs. There are two bottles of soda."

When she had finished, David went over and opened the refrigerator door slightly to get a peek first. He slammed the door and jumped back. "You were close," he said, "but you missed two things."

"Oh, do you mean the lunch meat and mayonnaise?" Tender asked.

I went over and opened the door. I checked the cream. It had expired a week ago. "How did you know all that?"

Tender puffed out her little chest. She liked to surprise people with what she knew, and she was proud of herself. "I know Dad likes jalapeño peppers, and he eats them right out of the jar." David and I just looked at each other.

"And here's how I know all these things. First, there were no fingerprints on the handle. That means you eat out most days. The last time you ate at home was over a week ago. There is dust on the handle but no fingerprints. You clean the house almost every week, but you have been too busy to do your regular cleaning."

"Tender," laughed David, "you are the funniest little girl I have ever met. Are you sure you're a child? I think you're a forty-year-old little person. How did you know what was in our fridge?"

"Easy. Everything had to be simple to make things to eat. I noticed grape jelly on the bottom corner of the toaster. I can smell jalapeño peppers. There are cake crumbs on the floor between the fridge and the counter. On the back of the countertop is a tiny piece of lunch meat and a drop of dried mayonnaise. So, you must have mayonnaise. The last time you cleaned there, your cloth must have jammed some lunch meat between the countertop and the tile."

I went over to the counter, took out a small knife, and picked out the piece of lunchmeat. I looked at Tender again and said, "You are amazing. But how about the bread? How did you know we had bread?"

Tender laughed. "Well, if you have jelly, I figured you would have bread to spread it on."

"And the hot dogs and hamburgers?" I asked.

"I saw a grill outside. I know you haven't lived here that long, but it already looks like you've used it a lot. You have a cookout once a month."

"How do you know that?" David asked in astonishment.

"Easy, I looked at your calendar," Tender grinned.

David threw up his hands. "I give up! You win, Sherlock. Let's have some breakfast; even child geniuses need to eat. What would you like?"

Tender yelled, "Cake."

"David," I admonished. "You can't ask a child her age what she wants to eat. Children her age need nutritious food."

"Aww, let her have cake just this once. She's been through a lot the last couple of days." David grinned, and I could see I was outvoted.

After breakfast, we headed to the police station. The car ride felt like an interrogation. Tender was thrilled to be visiting our workplace, and her questions revealed that she knew a startling amount of information about detective work. I answered her questions about fingerprinting and promised to take her fingerprints, but when she began asking about blood spatters, I'd had enough.

"Tender, that is not an appropriate topic of discussion for a little girl," I chided.

"Okay." She was silent for a minute. "Why don't you and David have any children?"

"That is also not an appropriate topic."

"Oh. I know why anyway, though. You can't have children. That is why you picked me. Now you have me, though. Aren't you so happy? I'm going to be your little girl now."

"Who helped you pick me, Tender?" I asked, curiously.

"My mommy."

"Yes, but how did she know all about us?"

Tender's face acquired a mulish look. "I can't tell you." She was silent for the last few minutes of the ride.

A stranger was sitting across from Chief Purdy at his desk. "Elaine, David this is Mrs. Johnstone, an official from a local orphanage. Nobody has come forward to claim Tender, and she does not match any descriptions of missing children. Mrs. Johnstone will take charge of her from here."

A whimper was issued from Tender, and she clung desperately to my leg. "Wait..." I looked at David, and he nodded encouragingly. "David and I would like to be Tender's foster parents, with the aim of adopting her, if possible."

Mrs. Johnstone smiled. "That certainly would be preferable. My secretary will call you this week to set up a home visit. In the meantime, Tender can remain in your custody."

After she left, Tender asked Chief Purdy if he was her new uncle. He laughed and nodded his head. Then he gave her a roll of Lifesavers and showed her how his handcuffs worked.

The following Monday, we made plans to see

an attorney and began the process of adoption. Later that day, we found ourselves in the office of a well-known child psychologist who had been recommended by Loriann's pediatrician.

"Mr. and Mrs. Purdy, you have a very unusual little girl here. She is one of the most intelligent—perhaps the most intelligent child I have ever worked with. I can't give you an exact score, as she scored off the charts for the tests, we use for children her age. She could certainly take a test that we use on older children, but the test would not be accurate, as it would not compare her to her peers."

"I gave *him* a test," Tender chirped.

"She did indeed," the man said with a smile. "Our test for young children involves recognizing patterns. Tender got bored with the test and started recalling all the patterns in reverse order. Then she decided to create some patterns to test me."

"So, do you think that Tender is gifted?" I asked.

The psychologist laughed. "Gifted? She is more than gifted. I would place her in the profound range. She is a very special girl."

I felt tears start in my eyes as I gave Tender a squeeze.

"Do you have any questions?" the psychologist asked.

"We are a bit overwhelmed right now," David

stated. "Any advice you could give us would be greatly appreciated."

"Well, in many ways, very gifted children are just like any other children. They need boundaries and discipline. Tender's intelligence is no replacement for your wisdom and guidance. Remember that she is a very young child." He paused. "You are going to be wonderful parents. Just trust your instincts."

On Saturday, a week later, I woke up early and discovered Tender's eyes were glued to my face. "Good morning, cutie pie. You really need to start sleeping in your own bed." So much for rules and boundaries.

She patted my cheek. "Mom, you are so pretty."

"So are you, darling." Tender put her head on my shoulder.

"Tender, I am confused. You look like a three-year-old, but you speak like an adult. How is that possible?" I asked.

"I am an adult." She giggled. "I'm forty-three years old. I just look little."

"My goodness!" I gasped in mock surprise. "You're older than I am. Maybe you're the mommy."

"No, you're the mommy. I'm the old little girl."

"You're so silly." I tickled her, and she giggled again.

"Tender," I heard David say from the other side

of the bed, "can you tell us more about your first mommy? Why did she pick us?"

"We both picked you. I wanted you because I like solving mysteries, just like you. And you don't drink alcohol, and you go to church. Does your church have a Sunday School? Does Anne go to Sunday School?"

Tender was very clever at changing the subject whenever we tried to pry into her mysterious origins. I sighed. Whatever the story was behind our little mystery girl, I was happy it had led her to us.

That evening, I had come to the realization that Tender had nothing appropriate to wear to church. David volunteered to drive over to Alex and Loriann's to borrow an outfit for Tender. I mentally added shopping for clothes to my to-do list. It was pouring rain, and David had just settled down in his pajamas, but he got dressed and headed out the door without protest. My knight in shining armor.

I also decided it was time for another bath for Tender. It was harder than I expected, and I felt horrible when I got a little soap in her eyes, and she cried. Fortunately, David walked in at just the right moment with a special surprise.

Anne had been so excited when David arrived to pick up Tender's outfit. "Uncle David is Tender going to be my new cousin?" she had asked. When he said yes, she shrieked, "Yeah!" and jumped from her chair to the couch and back again. Then she dashed to her room. She yanked open her closet and pulled out a lovely pink dress trimmed with lace and frills. "I want Tender to wear my princess dress so she can look pretty in church." she exclaimed.

When David arrived home with the dress, Tender's mouth dropped open at the sight of it, and her tears instantly dried up. We had a hard time convincing her that she couldn't wear the dress to bed.

Our Sunday morning tradition was to head for an early morning breakfast at the Eveready Diner and meet up with the rest of the Purdy family. Tender's eyes were enormous as we walked through the shiny doors.

"This is the best restaurant ever." she declared. Anne came over and took Tender by the hand, and the two giddy little girls sat together, giggling as they whispered in each other's ears. Tender thanked Anne for the dress. They were getting along just like sisters. "I wanted you to look beautiful at church today," Anne said. "It makes you look like a princess."

The entire Purdy family and several church friends sat together at a long table. There were stacks of pancakes, bowls of scrambled eggs, plates of bacon, and plenty of drinks like chocolate milk, orange juice, coffee, and every kind of pancake topping you could ever desire.

It was David's turn to pray. He cleared his throat. "Before I say the blessing, I'd like to introduce a new family member. This is Tender." After the prayer, everyone came over to our side of the table to hug Tender and welcome her to the family. I put my arm around her tiny shoulders, worried that she'd be overwhelmed by all the commotion. Everyone seemed to be talking at once. Tender whispered, "Mom, is this how big families act when they get together?"

"Yes," I said. "The Purdys are very chatty. Are you okay?"

"Yes, I love it, I want to eat breakfast here every day."

After we finished, we all went to church. There were two services; at 10 AM, the children attended Sunday School, and at 11 AM they joined the adults for the main service. I knew our social butterfly would enjoy Sunday School, but I worried about whether she would be able to sit still through the main service. Our pastor tended to run late, and he often did not finish up until 12:30.

To my surprise, Tender sat motionless and stared intently at the pastor the entire time he spoke. I noticed wrinkling on her forehead. After the service, as we were on our way to Jake and Louise's home, a small voice from the back seat asked, "Is it okay to correct Pastor Bob, or is that a sin?"

"Why, Tender? Did he make a mistake?" I asked.

She nodded. "He quoted Isaiah 53:11, but the verse was Isaiah 53:6: 'All we like sheep have gone astray,'" Tender said.

I was stunned. "Look it up," said David.

"He made a mistake," said Tender. "I liked his sermon though."

I sat staring at my open Bible. "David, she is correct." I looked at Tender and asked, "How would you know that?" Suddenly I wondered how many times I had said that in the past few days.

"My first mom wanted me to know about God, so I read the Bible." David and I looked at each other.

I said, "We need to read the Bible together as a family."

With her sweet smile beaming from the back seat of our car, Tender asked if she could do the reading, and we said she could. Her smile grew even bigger. "If we read three chapters a day, we can finish the Bible in one year," said Tender. "That's how long it took my first mom and I to read it."

As we pulled into the driveway of David's parents, Tender bounced excitedly in the back seat.

Before we entered, I knelt so I could see eye to eye with her. "Please stay with me until I tell you that you can go and play." I couldn't quite put my finger on why I was worried about Tender being away from me. Perhaps it was that she had come out of nowhere into our lives, and I was worried that she would disappear just as easily. Tender and I went around to everyone, giving kisses before we sat down for Sunday lunch. She loved all the attention. As soon as the table was cleared, Anne grabbed Tender by the hand, but before they could run off to play, Tender said she needed to speak to me first.

She tapped me on the arm. "Mom. Mom."

"Yes, darling," I said. "I will be with you in a minute." She had interrupted my conversation with David's mother about a recipe I wanted to get from her.

"Please, Mom, I have to tell you now!"

"Tender, it is not polite to interrupt. Please wait until I am finished talking."

Tender stomped her foot. I could see that something was wrong by the expression on her face. I excused myself as Tender took me by the hand and pulled me into an empty bedroom. As soon as the door closed behind us, she almost shouted, "Grandpa Purdy is sick. He will have a heart attack any minute."

I put my hands on her shoulders to help calm her. "Grandpa is fine, Tender. What put that into your head?"

"No, he's not fine. You must listen to me! We must take him to the hospital." Tender insisted.

As we returned to the living room, she dragged me over to my father-in-law, hoping that he would be able to reassure her.

"Grandpa, can I see your hands?" asked Tender. Grabbing his hands, she turned his palms up. "I noticed that when Grandpa held my hands, they were freezing."

Alex said, "So what? My hands are cold too."

I turned and glared at him. "Please let her finish. Continue, darling."

Tender gave a quick nod and said, "Well, then I noticed that his hands were turning dark blue, which means he has a blocked coronary artery, restricting blood flow to his heart."

"What can a three-year-old know about the heart?" Mary, David's sister, piped up in disbelief.

Knowing what the answer would be, I asked, "Tender, how do you know so much about the heart?"

Tender ignored me. "As we walked into the house," Tender said, "I noticed Grandpa rubbing his arm, and I'm worried that he might be having chest pains."

Now truly concerned, Louise turned to him and asked, "Jake, are you having chest pains?" He nodded.

"Call an ambulance! We need to get him to the closest hospital!" Louise said in a panic.

Minutes later, the ambulance team arrived and rushed him to Bismarck General Hospital. The whole family followed in their cars except for Louise, who had been allowed to ride in the ambulance. Once there, Jake was immediately brought into the operating room for emergency heart surgery. Everyone was amazed at how intelligent Tender was, and they asked her all kinds of difficult questions. She answered them all without hesitation.

I whispered in her ear, "Are you okay with all of these questions?"

"Oh yes, Mom; it's fun, and it helps keeps my mind busy," she replied.

After several hours of correcting the blockage, the heart surgeon came out to talk to us. Louise was so weak from crying that David and Alex helped her stand up and held her arms.

"My name is Dr. Arthur Turk. The good news is that your husband will make a full recovery. Your prompt reaction saved his life. If you had waited a few more hours to get him here, we would be facing a very different scenario." Everyone breathed a sigh of relief and looked at Tender.

"Doctor, my granddaughter noticed he was sick," Louise informed him.

"Well, let me shake her hand," Dr. Turk said. When Tender went forward, his mouth flew open.

"This is the granddaughter. How old are you, young lady?" he asked as he gave her a firm handshake.

"I am three years old, but I will be four next month," Tender informed him proudly.

"Can you tell me how you knew your grandpa was sick?" he asked. Tender went on to explain how she had diagnosed his condition.

"Hold on, sweetie." He took out his pad and pencil. "Okay, tell me again what you noticed."

When Tender had finished telling her story, he said, "You are a very observant little girl. How do you know so much?"

Tender explained that her biological mother had taken her to the library several times a week and that she had spent hours reading medical journals. The doctor looked more and more astonished.

"Tender is an unusual child," I explained.

"That is an understatement. Tender, next month I will be attending our annual national heart symposium. Would you like to go?"

Her eyes lit up. "How many doctors will be there?"

He laughed. "Hundreds. The best doctors in the country will all be there." He turned to me. "You can take as many guests as you please, and Tender may accompany you, if you think she is able to sit quietly."

"I'm *very* good at sitting still and listening." Tender promised.

I assured Dr. Turk that we would speak to Tender, and then our family would discuss his request and let him know. Before leaving, Louise hugged Tender. "Thank you for saving Grandpa," she said tearfully. Tender just smiled.

There was not much else we could do, as Louise was the only one allowed in his room until he was out of recovery. We all went home to pray and get a good night's sleep.

Before turning in for the night, I called in to the police station to let the sergeant know that David and I would be taking the next day off. We could take ten personal days a year, so fortunately it was not an issue.

Tender woke up very early on Monday. She was eager to visit Grandpa and see how he was doing. "We also have an appointment with the lawyer at 11 AM," said David. "Today, you officially become our little girl."

"Yes! That is very important," said Tender as she hugged us both. Then she added, "Sometime today, we need to talk."

"Do you want to talk now?" I asked.

Tender shook her head. "No, at the end of the day," she insisted.

We reached the hospital at about 9 AM and relieved Louise so that she could go home, get a shower, and rest. Alex was there to drive her home. I had called around and arranged for several Purdys to cover two-hour shifts visiting with Jake so Louise could get some time off.

When Tender entered the room, Jake smiled. "There she is—my little granddaughter who saved her grandpa's life." She grinned, and Jake asked her to sit on the edge of his bed.

We talked for the next hour and a half, and then we had to leave. David's sister, Mary, would take the next shift. We arrived at our attorney's office just in time, but he didn't call us in for another thirty minutes.

After reviewing Tender's documents, the attorney, Jason Young, said, "Well, everything seems in order. The attorney who designed this legal document didn't leave anything out."

Tender interrupted and touched his arm with her small hand. "Can I guess what you are going to say next?"

"Go ahead," the attorney said. "Give it a try, but I doubt you will guess."

"She is a little detective," I said. "She loves to guess things."

"Okay," Tender continued. "You will make a copy of the original documents. Then my parents will sign both, and you will sign as a notary public. You will then put the original documents in the envelope supplied and send it to the post office, noting 'sign as received.' If the mail gets lost before it reaches New York, Mom and Dad could forfeit their right to become my parents."

The attorney looked impressed. "That is a big word for a little girl. You already talk like a lawyer. How would you like to be my assistant?" he joked.

"No, thank you. I'm going to be a detective. I'm not done, though. Within the next few days, our attorney will send a response letter, informing the attorney who represents me and my first mother that you have signed and sent all the legal documents required for guardianship of me. That information will be signed and notarized by you and this attorney. How did I do?"

"You sound like a law student, but you look like I should give you a lollipop." The attorney was amazed.

"I have one more request, please," Tender asked.

"What is your request, young lady?"

"There is a blank space for my middle name. Can I have a middle name?" Tender asked.

"Sure. How about Hepzibah? Or Gomer? Gomer is a nice name," the attorney teased.

Tender scowled. "I know those are Bible names, but they are awful. I want to be called Louise, like my new grandma. I love her."

"Louise is a beautiful name, Tender. Your new mother and father need to officially make the request to me," the attorney said, looking over at us.

"Okay, I would like my daughter to have the name of Tender Louise Purdy." David took a step back and gave Tender a big hug, with tears in his eyes.

We were excited to sign all the paperwork, but Mr. Young needed to make the copies first. He gave Tender the largest lollipop in his treat jar and said, "Please report back at 2 PM, and I will have everything ready for you to sign and mail."

We were starving, so we went out to eat at Ashley's Pizzeria. After eating, we still had another hour to kill.

"What should we do for the next hour?" David asked. It was not worth going home, as it was a thirty-minute drive.

I reminded him that our little girl needed a bed,

and we headed over to Sears and Roebuck. Tender was so excited and kept asking, "Am I going to get a big-girl bed?"

"Yes, you are, my darling girl, but I want you to have a safety rail," I said firmly.

"I can live with that," she agreed. "My very first big-girl bed."

Once we arrived, it didn't take Tender long to pick out a beautiful twin bed. It had a white headboard with a floral design in the middle. The footboard had pink legs, and the middle of the bed was white. It took longer to pick out a mattress, as Tender had to try them all twice before choosing. Every mattress was either "too hard" or "too soft," but finally our Goldilocks found one that was "just right." The bed would be delivered in two days.

We were late getting back to the attorney; David and I signed all the documents and were given all three envelopes with instructions. We headed to the post office, sending the most important one of the three as certified mail. A signature from the post office was required. Over the next two days, David would mail the other letters.

On the way home, we stopped by the hospital and found that Louise had just returned from a walk. Jake looked tremendous and wanted to go home, but the hospital had a rule that patients had to stay for five days after major surgery. Therefore, he could not leave until Friday morning. Louise wanted to know if we had signed the papers, and then Jake did something we would never have expected. He took Tender by the hands and spoke.

"Tender, did those two sign those papers yet? If not, Grandpa is going to sign them!" He laughed.

Tender gave her grandpa a big hug and said, "Grandpa, I love you so much." We all laughed and kissed Jake goodbye as we left.

"Don't forget to send me the bill for my new granddaughter's bed and sheets." He called after us.

Out in the hallway, Tender suddenly shouted, "Grandma, we have the same name now!" Louise was teary-eyed when we explained what she meant. She took Tender and whispered into her ear, and Tender gave her the longest hug. Of course, David had to know what his mom had said, but Tender just shook her head and smiled.

We headed back to Sears to purchase bed sheets, a pink bedspread, and pink blankets. We also picked up several more outfits for Tender, including dress-up clothes as well as casual and play clothes. Shopping for her was such fun. Finally, before heading home, we stopped at our favorite hamburger restaurant. Then we went home, as we were all exhausted from a long day.

As we came in the door, I said, "Okay, young lady, let's brush your teeth and get to bed." Tender asked if she could wear her new pajamas. I replied, "Yes, of course."

Tender hugged the soft, fluffy garments. "I've never had brand-new clothes. All my pajamas were worn by other little girls first."

David came into her room to say good night. We tucked her in and kissed her. As we were about to leave, she said, "Wait! Come back; we need to talk. I have something to tell you."

"All right, sweetie; you can tell us, but then you need to go to sleep."

"I know you are going to try to find out who my attorney is."

"Of course, we are, darling. We need to find out more about your first mother."

"It doesn't matter. I'm Tender Louise Purdy now. Please don't try to find out. You will mess everything up."

David responded, "But Tender, we need to know who the attorney is. You need to trust us to handle this. I know you are very smart, but you are still a little girl, and we are grown-ups—"

"Stop, and please listen," Tender interrupted. "It is very complicated. You will never be able to figure everything out. I would tell you everything

Tender Answers the Call

if I thought it would help, but it wouldn't. Please promise."

David finally agreed to leave things as they were, at least for a while. Then we left the room and went into the living room to relax for a while before going to bed. Just before falling asleep, I mentioned to David that it was sometimes hard to remember we were talking to a child.

David, Tender, and I were off to the police station in the morning. Next to the police station was a private daycare where we planned to drop off Tender before our shifts began. The owner of the daycare, Mrs. Alice Hall, had been told ahead of time about how bright Tender was. After only one day, Mrs. Hall said she needed help to keep this smart little girl occupied. We asked Tender what she would like to do while at the daycare. She answered that she had noticed all our college books on criminal justice, and she wanted to study them.

Later, when everything was quiet, I told David that I was not sure a child should be reading about criminal justice.

"Honey, I agree, but Tender's brain is not that of an almost-four-year-old. She has a curious mind," he replied.

"But David," I continued, "she *is* a child. What

advantage is there in allowing her to study criminal justice?"

"For one thing, she is always the smartest person in the room. She could help us on cases in which we hit a roadblock."

By morning, we had agreed to allow her access to all our college textbooks, one book at a time. We told her that we would need to discuss it with her before she went on to another textbook. She was so happy to learn all about what her parents did for a living.

We spoke to Alice Hall before daycare started, and she set aside a special reading space for Tender. Tender would be allowed to spend some time every day reading our college textbooks, but she was not allowed to show them to the other children.

When I picked up Tender after daycare, she was ready to talk about what she had read. "I know you were worried that it would frighten me, but it didn't. I understand that sometimes there are bad people in the world. I solved the case at the end of the chapter. It was easy."

"Can you remind us of what the case was about?" David asked.

"It involved a three-year-old, like me," Tender said. "When the mother went in to care for her in the morning, she was gone. Her window was locked.

Tender Answers the Call

The house had an alarm system, with motion detectors still set. And they had a dog. Okay, Mom, don't tell me what your professor said. Tell me what you thought when you read it."

"Okay—I thought the child had left the house by herself, undetected, because the motion detectors were set higher for adults, not for a child. I concluded that she left the house on her own."

"Good guess, and I suppose since I don't know what the professor's answer was, that could be correct," Tender said thoughtfully.

She then turned to David. "Dad, what was your conclusion?"

"Well, since the father was estranged from his family, I thought he entered the house and shut the alarm off, took the three-year-old, and reset the alarm on his way out."

"Also very good, and maybe the correct answer," Tender said.

When David asked her what she thought, Tender replied, "The father hired a professional burglar who knew how to enter an alarmed home. The father had explained the alarm system. The burglar took the ladder from the back of the shed and placed it under the child's window. He quietly climbed up to the window and took out a strong magnet. By sliding the magnet from right to left, he could unlatch the lock. He removed the child wearing gloves and a cloth mask, closed the window, and relocked it by sliding the strong magnet from left to right. He went down the ladder and brought the child to the father, took his money, and left."

"I guess you're right. Who have you been talking to?" I exclaimed.

"Nobody! I figured it out all by myself," Tender beamed. "I noticed when the hired professional used the magnet to close the latch, it was only half closed. A window latch is easy to open, much harder to close," Tender finished with a smile.

***

Our first month with Tender went by fast. Before we knew it, it was her fourth birthday. We threw a big party, and almost everyone gave her jigsaw puzzles. David and I gave her a doll carriage and a tea set, which included many pieces of blue plastic: four trios of cups, saucers, and teaspoons, as well as a teapot, sugar bowl, and cream jug. We had both noticed that Tender, despite being a little adult in some respects, still loved playing with her doll. I was hoping that the present would help David remember she was a child. Her favorite present was given to her by Grandpa Purdy, who was now fully recovered. When he rolled it out, Tender jumped into his arms. "Thank you, Grandpa and Grandma! I love you both."

"You're welcome," replied Grandma. "Let's see if it's the right size."

It was a Schwinn 12-inch Midget Coppertone bike with training wheels. It was perfect for Tender.

Finally, we gave her our surprise present. Tender unwrapped the box with care and opened it. Inside was a letter from her attorney in New York. Tender read it aloud.

Dear Mr. and Mrs. Purdy and Tender,

I am pleased to inform you that your dossier has been received and has been recorded in the certificate of birth records. A new birth certificate has been awarded to Tender Louise Purdy, born on August 3, 1960. Her father is listed as David Paul Purdy, and her mother is listed as Elaine Purdy. Congratulations, Tender Louise Purdy. And thank you, Mr., and Mrs. Purdy. Remember, Tender you know how to contact me if you have an emergency. May God bless you.

Tender jumped up, kissed her new birth certificate, and then kissed us. David and I both had tears in our eyes. Everyone at the party clapped and cheered, especially her Aunt Mary. The party went late into the night, as the Purdy family loved playing games. The men weren't so thrilled because we ladies had Tender on our team. They complained it wasn't fair we had Tender. My only response was to ask if they were afraid of a four-year-old.

All the men responded, "Yes!" Everybody laughed.

That evening, at home, we gave Tender a letter from her first mom.

My dear Tender,

Happy fourth birthday. By now, if all went as planned, you are Tender Purdy from Bismarck, North Dakota. I have been watching over you from heaven. I pray you are happy with your new mom and dad. I have also enclosed some money for you to purchase a present from me.

My dear Tender, over the next year I want you to help one person whom you have never met before and who is in trouble. If you agree, please send a letter to your attorney in secret. I trust your mom and dad will honor your request for privacy. I have never loved anyone more than I loved you, Tender.

Dear Elaine, please read the note addressed to you and David contained inside the envelope;

it will explain what I think Tender will enjoy from her first mom.

Love,
Your mom in heaven.

Once in my bedroom, I read the letter from Tender's mom:

Dear Elaine and David,

Thank you for loving Tender. I am sure she has turned your life upside down, but I hope for the better. Enclosed is enough money to buy Tender some camping gear and camping clothes. My only request is you both take her (and maybe a friend) camping on a night in which she can enjoy the stars. Astronomy was the only subject she had no interest in. I am hoping one of you loves the stars and can show her the beauty of God's creation.

Tender's present is at Bismarck's Shasta Recreational Vehicles. It has been paid for in full and registered under David Purdy. Also, you are booked for this weekend at the Bismarck KOA Campground. Thank you both and have fun.

David and I both had tears in our eyes. "This is just like a fairy tale," I whispered.

We looked at each other. "I guess we are going camping," I said after a pause.

"Finally, something we know more about than Tender," laughed David.

The next day was a Thursday. After work, David headed over to claim Tender's new RV. He signed a few papers and was given the title and registration. He needed Alex to help him tow it with his truck to our house, and he invited Alex, Loriann, and Anne to join us for a weekend campout. The trailer slept four and was beautiful: pink and blue, Tender's favorite colors.

Camping was more fun than I thought it would be. Everyone except Tender and I had slept out under the stars many times. Alex and David showed us how to cook hot dogs on a stick over the campfire, and later we roasted marshmallows.

As we all laid on blankets looking up at the stars, I couldn't help but think about Tender's first mom. Alex showed us Orion, the Hunter; Pegasus, the Flying Horse; Ursa Major, the Great Bear; Leo, the Lion; Canis Major, the Great Dog; as well as Cancer, Hercules, and Pisces. Tender was so excited about her new "friends" in the sky that nothing short of a brand-new RV could have tempted her to say goodbye to them. We girls slept in the trailer, and the men slept in a tent outside in sleeping bags.

Tender Answers the Call

After only an hour, Alex knocked on the camper and asked us if there was any room for him, as he was being bitten by giant mosquitoes. Loriann cracked the door open and handed him bug lotion.

"Alex, where is David?" Loriann asked.

"Sleeping," he replied.

"Good night, dear; no room in the inn. Love you." Loriann said.

"I doubt it, or you would let me in." Alex complained, as the door shut.

Tender and Anne fell asleep early, and Loriann and I talked for a while.

On Saturday, David and Alex had all kinds of fun games for us to play: Frisbee (Tender reminded us that it was invented by Fred Morrison in 1957) and Wiffle ball, with paper plates for bases. Everyone enjoyed that the most.

Anne asked Tender who invented the Wiffle ball, and for some reason, Tender sat on the ground and put her hands over her face for several minutes.

"Honey, are you okay?" I asked.

Tender put up one finger, then dramatically stood up. "I needed to use my recall. It was David Mullany from Fairfield, Connecticut, in 1953, and he designed it for his twelve-year-old son."

On the way home the next day the car was quiet, as everyone was exhausted. When we arrived at home, we discovered a formal invitation in the mail. We decided to allow Tender to attend the National Heart Symposium the following week.

SIX

Tender Makes New Friends

David, Jake, Louise, Tender, and I all attended the symposium together. When we arrived at the symposium, we were greeted by Dr. Turk.

"Hello, Elaine. I'm so happy that you decided to bring Tender. I'm presenting some of my research today, and I would like to call Tender onstage to answer a few questions. Would you be all right with that? You can stay right by her side the whole time."

Then he turned to Tender. "Don't be nervous, Tender. I will just be asking you some questions about the day you saved your grandpa's life."

"Nervous? I'm the one who will be nervous." I exclaimed. I was shaking. Tender took my hand and squeezed it.

"Mrs. Purdy, you will do fine," Dr. Turk continued. "You and Tender will be on first after lunch.

Please do not tell anyone Tender is the one being interviewed. No one knows how old my special guest is."

Tender enjoyed all the morning classes. Dr. Turk told me to pretend I was Dr. Elaine Purdy and that I had brought my four-year-old daughter to the symposium because my babysitter had a personal emergency at the last minute.

Lunch was delicious, and when it was finished, it was time for Tender and me to mount a stage in public for the first time. I asked if she was nervous, and of course, she wasn't.

To begin the afternoon session, Dr. Turk announced, "I am going to tell you a true story. My father was a salesman all his working life; he encouraged my younger brother and me to reach for the stars. He never made much money. We had a modest little two-bedroom home in the country. My dad only got paid once a month, on the first of each month. I was born on July 7, and my younger brother, Ken, was born twelve months and fourteen days later, on July 21. If my dad had good sales in the month of June, we would receive birthday presents, but often, we never received gifts.

"One year, on my tenth birthday, Dad had had a very good June. I was so excited because I had been dreaming of a new bicycle. I was very disappointed when Dad brought out a box for me to open. I was so confused when I saw it was full of hundreds of parts: tires, screws, bolts, a chain, handlebars, a seat, and too many others to mention.

My dad and I were about to discover something no one in the family knew. As I spread all the parts on the living room floor, Dad just looked at me in fear. 'I should have had the store assemble it,' he said sadly. I stared at blueprints only an engineer could decipher. A bitter tear slid down my cheek, and I crumpled the blueprints and threw them across the room."

"Just then, my younger brother, Ken, walked into the room and grabbed the blueprints as they flew through the air. He flattened them out and just looked over them for no more than ten minutes. Then he put them down, never to look at them again, and walked out of the room. He returned a few minutes later, with Dad's dusty toolbox—more Mom's toolbox, really, as Dad was not good at fixing things. One hour later, with not one bolt or screw left out, my red and gold bike was finished. Two weeks later, when his bike arrived, it was a Schwinn like mine, except green and white. He assembled it in less than thirty minutes. He would go on to be an engineer. These bikes would be lifesavers for my brother and me, as we had walked three miles to our one-room school five days a week. Thanks to my brother, we rode our bikes until we went off to college."

At that point, one of the workers wheeled out a slightly faded red-and-gold Schwinn bicycle. Everyone stood and clapped.

"My next guest is also going to put a smile on your face. Without further ado, I present Miss Tender Louise Purdy, and her mother, Mrs. Elaine Purdy."

Tender walked out on the big stage, her back straight, her smile beaming. She marched across the stage holding my hand, and we sat down on a very comfortable couch. Dr. Turk sat in a chair close to Tender, looking out at the crowd, and Tender waved happily. The auditorium was packed with over two thousand doctors and administrators.

Dr. Turk handed Tender her own microphone. "The reason I told you the story of my brother is because he has a photographic memory, and I have never met anyone else who has this gift, until I met Tender Purdy. Tender, why don't you introduce yourself and the lady with you here today?"

Tender spoke fearlessly. "Good afternoon, everyone. I would like to introduce you to my mom, Detective Elaine Purdy. If you have any intentions of giving a four-year-old a hard time, I would like to remind you that she has handcuffs." Everyone laughed, surprised to hear a four-year-old child speaking so articulately. Tender could hear the buzz. I waved and smiled at the crowd.

"Tender, I was told you like to read medical journals. Is that true?" questioned Dr. Turk.

"Yes; The *BMJ* is a medical journal first published on October 3, 1840, but I have only read the *BMJ*, or *The British Medical Journal*, going back to 1948." Tender looked up at me. I just smiled and held her hand.

"Do you mean you have read every one?" pressed Dr. Turk.

"It is hard to get copies of them all, but I have read hundreds," Tender replied.

"Tender, can you tell us why you are here today?" asked Dr. Turk, smiling at Tender.

"I was invited here after saving my grandpa, whom I love, from having a heart attack," said Tender seriously.

"Can you tell us how it all started?" he asked.

"It was Sunday after church, and we were all enjoying our family lunch at my grandpa and grandma's house. You know, no one cooks like Grandma. I knew you were thinking I was going to say Grandpa."

The crowd erupted in laughter again. Tender

looked at me. "Boy, Mom, this is an easy crowd." she quipped.

When the laughter quieted, she continued. "When I went over to Grandpa to hug and kiss him, I noticed that something was wrong, and I decided to tell Mom. I could've gone to Dad, but he was watching football, and it would have gone something like this. 'Dad, I wanted to let you know Grandpa is having a heart attack.' 'Okay, my darling daughter, as soon as the game is over, we all can go for ice cream.' "

The crowd started clapping, laughing, and yelling. Dr. Turk slapped his leg in laughter.

"I went over to Mom and informed her that Grandpa was having a heart attack and we needed to get him to the hospital. I explained the symptoms he was having," Tender continued.

"What did you notice?" asked Dr. Turk.

"I noticed his hands were freezing. Grandpa told me his hands were always cold, but they were never that cold. I also noticed his hands and lips were turning blue. That meant a lack of oxygen. He also had shortness of breath, and he felt lightheaded. For those who are just interns, that means he felt dizzy." At this, the crowd stood up, clapping, laughing, and cheering.

"I asked Grandpa if he felt tired and if he had heartburn, indigestion, or pain around the stomach area. I also asked if he felt any nausea. I would have said 'throw up,' but I didn't want to upset any of you doctors who have sensitive stomachs." The crowd was enjoying Tender.

"The final signs that my grandpa was not just feeling under the weather, like he thought, was that he was getting chest pains, and he was also complaining about his jaw aching. I also noticed he was panting for air like an asthmatic. By the way, my grandpa does not have asthma."

Tender ended her story by thanking all the wonderful medical care staff for their service and for saving her grandpa. Then Tender pointed to the side stage. "Ladies and gentlemen, my grandpa is alive and well."

The crowd stood and clapped and cheered. For the next two hours, David, Jake, Louise, and I enjoyed watching as Tender answered every question the doctors threw at her, no matter how difficult. I think every pediatrician at the symposium wanted to be Tender's doctor. But when her pediatrician, Dr. Nancy Henderson, came up to say hi, Tender jumped up and gave her a hug. After that, the other doctors knew they had no chance. I think almost every doctor gave her a business card. If it wasn't for Jake getting tired, they would have kept us there all day and night.

On the way home, Tender fell asleep in the car, exhausted. She had made so many new friends that day, and her life would never be the same.

Over the next few weeks, I set her up with a Rolodex system, with one section for doctors, one for family, one for church, and one for friends. The ones she was most proud of were her friends on the police force. Tender was surprised by how many relatives we had that didn't have the name of Purdy. I explained to her that when her Aunt Mary would get married, she would change her name to her new husband's last name. She was happy to have so many new cousins in her family Rolodex too.

Tender kept us on our toes, and she always surprised us. She completed all our college studies in criminal justice. She also completed every jigsaw puzzle the family owned, in record time. David and I had a slow year in cases, but when we got stuck on a case, we would discuss the case with Tender and have her help us.

During this year, Tender would often act as the family doctor for consultations. She was also the neighbors' go-to person for all kinds of information about school and medical problems. She loved being kept busy helping others.

I was concerned about daycare again this year. Tender needed to be challenged. How could I find a school that could educate a four-year-old genius? I was also worried that Tender would be smarter than the teacher, so I contacted the superintendent of the Bismarck School Department and set up an appointment for the following week.

My meeting was with Superintendent Maria Angelino. I explained that Tender had an IQ of 180 and told her about all of Tender's accomplishments at her age.

Mrs. Angelino informed me that my daughter was not the only genius to come their way. "Mrs. Purdy, let me tell you a story. In early 1913, two geniuses founded a school for gifted children because they could not get the special education they needed when they were children. Narcissa Cox Vanderlip and Frank A. Vanderlip started the nearby Montessori School. That is the place we recommend for gifted children."

This was exciting news. "Where are they located?" I asked.

Mrs. Angelino wrote the address down and handed it to me. I was surprised it was nearby in Bismarck. It was called the Montessori School for Children.

When I contacted the school, they asked me to bring Tender in to be tested. They were not concerned about her age. The test was going to be on Saturday, just a few days away. Because of her age, I would be allowed to remain in the back of the room just in case my daughter needed me.

Tender was excited to take the test. The test proctor was Principal Adler, who was also responsible for the interviews. "Children," Mrs. Adler began, "you are being asked to take the most difficult test offered in the United States. It is called the Scholastic Aptitude Test, or SAT. The test covers math, problem-solving, reading, and writing. You will have three hours to complete your test. You may get up at any time and go to your parent if you have a need."

Within one hour, most students started taking a break. At approximately one hour and ten minutes, Tender got up.

"Hi, honey," I said, "do you need a break?"

Tender said yes at first, then she said that we could leave. "What? Have you finished already?" I raised my eyebrows.

"Yes." Tender replied. I told her to take her test up to Mrs. Adler.

When Tender took up her test, Mrs. Adler looked at her watch. "You are finished?" she asked.

Tender replied that she was. Mrs. Adler looked at me and told me that was the fastest time a test had ever been completed.

Tender Answers the Call

Three days later, I hadn't heard any response from the Montessori School or from Mrs. Adler. But on the following day, I received a letter, asking me to come to the school next Saturday morning for a consultation.

When Saturday arrived, every scenario was going through my head the entire morning. This time, David accompanied me. Tender was having a playdate with her cousin Anne, which we had arranged for every Saturday. I was concerned that she needed more companionship with children her age. Anne's neighborhood friends also joined in the fun.

As we went into Principal Adler's office, we saw that there were several other teachers present who introduced themselves. Mrs. Adler asked us both to sit. I spoke up.

"First, I am so sorry that Tender most likely didn't finish her test."

"Why would you think she didn't?" asked Mrs. Adler.

"Well, she turned it in so quickly, I thought she must not have finished it all."

"Oh, she finished, all right," said Mrs. Adler. "She received the highest score any student has received at our school. A perfect score of 1600!"

David and I just looked at each other in shock.

One of the other teachers said, "We are so excited to instruct Tender in things that interest her."

Mrs. Adler informed us that at this school, they didn't try to teach any subjects a student is already proficient in. "We look outside the box and discover what she may not know."

I asked what grade she would be in.

"She will not be in any grade," Mrs. Adler replied. "Most likely, we will be teaching her college-level studies. These are some of the studies we will be exploring: advanced biology, world history, law, astronomy, accounting, physics, advanced math, and all the sciences."

Mrs. Adler went on to tell us that the first day of school would be September 4. Then she said, "Mrs. Purdy, at 7:30 AM that day, please bring Tender to classroom 11A. That is where you will drop her off every day. You can pick her up at 4 PM in the same classroom. If you cannot drop her off or pick her up, you must register any individual who is allowed to pick her up. You may go now to the main office to fill out the paperwork."

We went to the office and registered ourselves, Tender's grandparents, and Aunt Mary. We also planned to pay for her first month's tuition, but we were surprised to discover it was already paid in full for the whole year. Tender also had a running tab for all her books and a meal ticket for lunches. David and I were stunned!

When we tried to find out who paid the bill, we discovered that a certified check had been made out to the Montessori School for Tender's account. This made us even more determined than ever to try to find out what was going on.

After we finished, we went to enjoy lunch and discuss what had just transpired. We decided not to let Tender know how she did on the test. At the end of the day, we picked her up and went out to eat at her favorite restaurant, serving the biggest burger in the world.

"Tender, darling," I said. "We were wondering who would have paid for all of your school bills."

"I understand you must be confused," Tender said, "but I promised my first mom not to give you any information regarding my benefactor."

At home, we found a letter in the mail; the stamp indicated that it came from New York City. We opened the letter, and I read it to David and Tender:

Dear Mr. and Mrs. Purdy

As you must now realize, Tender has a benefactor who would like to remain anonymous. This benefactor knows everything that is happening in Tender's life. He would like to thank you for loving her and welcoming her into your family. We are delighted that Tender noticed a serious problem with David's father and saved his life. If you feel Tender needs anything, let her contact me at my law office. Please honor her benefactor's wishes and do not try to work out this mystery. God bless you both.

SEVEN

Tender Is Needed

Monday was the first day of school, and my big girl, now four years old, was so excited. I delivered her to room 11A. I don't know why, but I started to cry as I handed her a treat for the 10 AM break time. I also gave her a piece of fruit for the afternoon break. Drinks would be supplied at school.

Tender hugged me and said, "Mom, don't cry, please." Then she smiled and skipped into her classroom.

I cried all the way to the police station. What was wrong with me? Loriann had been right when she said to bring some extra tissues on the first day.

As I entered the station, I discovered David was working on our unsolved case. Each team was given one unsolved case if there was nothing new to work on. I asked him what this one was about.

"A bank robbery that took place last August," David replied.

Looking at the photo in the file, David and I didn't notice anything that could help us identify the two men caught by the camera. They both wore gorilla Halloween masks.

David and I studied the case for hours before going to lunch. Just as we got our food, we got a call to report to a home address in Bismarck. We left immediately and headed over to the address. We never did get to eat lunch. Upon arriving, we saw several police cars, with one blocking the street. We identified ourselves and entered the house. The chief informed us that we would be the lead investigators.

"Please fill us in," I requested.

The chief began the briefing. "About noon, Anthony Russo was picked up at school by his mom. He is in the morning kindergarten class. When they got home, Anthony went into the yard to play on the swings. The yard is totally fenced, and the only gate is locked. His mother was making lunch for him. When she went to call him in, he was gone."

David went right into action. He gathered everyone on his team. "Get upstairs and take photos from every window, front, sides, and back," he ordered. "Take photos of every inch of the yard and fence, but don't step on the lawn," he demanded.

Tender Answers the Call

He asked the chief whether he had helicopters taking photos of the neighborhood. The chief answered that this had been completed already.

Meanwhile, I interviewed the mother. The father was on his way home. "Mrs. Russo, we will do everything in our power to find Anthony," I assured her. She could not stop crying.

"I am going to ask you a few questions," I said in the gentlest voice possible. "Did you hear any unusual sounds? You can just nod or shake your head." She shook her head no. "Did you see anything unusual?" She shook her head no, again.

We had no leads, and we knew we had just twelve hours to find Anthony before the odds of locating him went down. David and I headed back to the station. As pictures surfaced from the darkroom, we began to tack up the pictures on a corkboard as they came in. Next to the corkboard was a chalkboard on which I started to write any information we had.

Soon all the pictures were on the corkboard. First, we viewed the helicopter pictures. Nothing seemed out of the ordinary in the photos. The entire team of twenty officers and six FBI agents studied each shot. How did the perpetrator enter the property? There were no footprints in the yard except for the child's. His dad had mowed the lawn last night, and because it rained, even Mr. Russo's prints were gone.

The local news showed Anthony's picture and his mom pleading with the abductors. There will be a $5,000 reward for the safe return of Anthony, no questions asked.

I went over to David and whispered, "I think we should get Tender over here. She may not see anything that we don't, but she might." David agreed that we needed to find this boy soon, so we headed to the school and had Tender released early.

On the way back to the station, I explained to her what had happened. As we entered the station, everyone wondered why Tender was there. When she came into the investigation room, David put a rolling chair close to the corkboard for her.

With a huge scowl on his face, one of the FBI agents demanded to know what was going on. We told him about Tender's ability to solve puzzles, but he didn't let up.

"Why would you bring your daughter? Who brings a child into the investigation room? She can't be more than four or five years old."

After listening to him for a while, Tender turned around. "For a few minutes, I have been observing this FBI agent." She nodded her head toward him. "I can tell that you and your wife are separated and that you are sleeping on someone's couch. You had hot dogs for lunch."

"Who told you that?" the agent yelled. It seemed impossible, but he looked even more angry.

"You did." said Tender.

"What are you talking about?" he snapped.

"You only left last night because you had a huge argument with your wife. One of these agents allowed you to sleep on their couch. I noticed your shirt is only wrinkled on the side that you slept on. You had hot dogs for lunch, and you had mustard on your tie. Should I say why you were late getting to the police station?"

"No! That will be enough." he shouted and moved his chair as far away from Tender as he could.

Tender nodded and turned back to the pictures. She reviewed all the pictures and then said, "Okay, I know who took the boy." Tender smiled.

David said, "Please go ahead, Tender."

"Is the mother here?" Tender asked. David nodded.

"Please bring her in," said Tender.

David went to collect Mrs. Russo, letting her know that his daughter had a question for her. She looked puzzled, as did the FBI agents.

After Mrs. Russo was settled, Tender asked, "Did you hear a hammer banging in nails at noon?"

"Yes, I did," the mom replied. "But what does that have to do with my son?"

Tender then turned around and pointed to the corner of the fence near the swing. "Mom, do you see it?"

I shook my head no. "Three boards have been removed and then reinstalled, but they are not installed like the rest of the fence," Tender said. "Two are a little lower, and one is higher."

David removed the photo and showed it to everyone. Then he said, "Now we know why there were no footprints at the locked gate. So, Tender, can you tell us where Anthony is?"

"Yes," Tender replied. "See the overhead photos that show the neighborhood? There is a moving truck in front of this house, just a few blocks away. Find that truck, and you will find the boy."

Within 30 minutes, the FBI had a warrant to search the house where the moving truck had been seen. We also had the plate number for the moving truck given to us by the rental company. The truck would not be hard to find. The FBI notified all the state and local police to be on the lookout for a rental truck with the North Dakota plate number the rental company had given us.

A few hours later, the good news came that the kidnappers had stopped at a café in Mandan, North

Tender Answers the Call

Dakota. Local police arrested Douglas and Melissa Wind without incident, and they had Anthony safely with them. Everyone started to clap, and three hours later, mother, father, and son were reunited.

Tender looked up at me and asked, "We did well?"

"You did great." I said. "You just helped save that boy's life."

"I like police work, and my mom in heaven would be proud of me today." Tender exclaimed and laughed.

One of the FBI agents asked Tender, David, and me if we could come to FBI headquarters to speak to Director Lance. I looked at Tender and asked if she would like to go. She did, so I suggested that we go after school on the day after tomorrow.

Before we left, Agent Sisson asked to speak to Tender in private. They went out in the hallway.

"What should I do next?" he asked looking desperate.

"You need to apologize and tell your wife you will go to AA for help with your drinking problem."

"How did you know I drink?" Sisson asked with furrowed brows.

"I have a strong sense of smell." Tender informed the agent, who gave her a weak smile.

Tender continued. "First, I want you to enroll

in AA so you can convince your wife that you are serious, and then she might take you back. Next, once you are home, have a booze party."

"I thought you wanted me to stop drinking!" Sisson exclaimed.

"I have read a lot about addictions," Tender explained. "I recommend that you pour all your alcoholic beverages down the sink. Invite everyone you have hurt with your drinking and ask for forgiveness."

Agent Sisson hugged her and told her she was amazing.

Tender then said, "Don't let me down. I will pray for you, Agent Sisson."

When Tender rejoined her parents, she said, "Let's go, Mom and Dad. I'm hungry."

We were too, so we picked up pizza at Ashley's Pizzeria on the way home. David and I told Tender how proud we were of her.

"Tender," David asked, "what did Agent Sisson want to talk about?"

Tender replied, "That is between him and me. We talked about something I said to him when we met, but I can't share much. My first mom taught me that God delights in those who don't spread gossip. She was very wise."

"Tender, earlier today, we received an unsolved

case from last August to work on. Would you be willing to look at the evidence we acquired?" I asked.

"Yes, Mom; as soon as we arrive home." Tender replied. She was excited to work on another case so soon.

I was still not sure we should be asking our daughter to get involved with criminal cases, but she seemed to enjoy helping us find Anthony Russo. As we approached home, I turned around to look at Tender and ask her a question. "Darling, if your dad and I decided you were too young to be involved in our cases, what would you say?"

"I would say that God has blessed me with a gift to see the outcome to a puzzle put in front of me. I love solving mysteries and putting bad people behind bars. If you had to deny me something that I love, I would be fine but disappointed. Mom, are you going to stop me?" Tender asked as she looked me in the eyes.

"I guess not," I answered as David pulled into the driveway. Tender smiled happily.

We entered the house and sat down at the kitchen table. Tender took out her favorite magnifying glass and started reviewing the evidence.

"Dad, can we call this the 'gorilla mask' case?" Tender asked.

"That sounds good," David replied.

"Well, I noticed that both these gorillas were about the same height and build. I also noticed they both had olive-tone skin. I believe they were either brothers or twins, most likely of Spanish or Mexican descent. I also have a hunch these two gorillas work at the bank, maybe as a cleaning crew or as maintenance workers. They most likely have worked for the bank for years and are planning to move back to their home country. Find the brothers, and you will find the robbers."

Tender said she was tired, so she grabbed me by the hand as we headed to her bedroom. She put on her pajamas and then brushed her teeth. I called David in so he could say good night. As we do every night, I started reading a Bible story; this night's reading was from the book of John. Within fifteen minutes, David tapped my shoulder, as our little girl had fallen asleep. We both gave her a kiss on her cheek and headed to the living room to discuss the case.

"David, I believe they may have robbed several other banks." "Why do you think that?" asked David. "They seem to know their way around banks very well. Who would suspect someone that works at the bank to then rob that bank," I replied.

The next morning before we left to take Tender to school we told her what we had discussed last night. She told us to find out where they had worked before and to find out if that bank had also been robbed.

Later we took Tender to school and headed to police headquarters to inform Chief Purdy what Tender had discovered. He contacted Judge Larson, who granted us a specific warrant to search all employee records. The branch manager, Kyle Fleming, was surprised but very cooperative. He took us to a back room where all the files were located, and he instructed one of the ladies working at a desk to assist us. Her name was Susan Cantone. She was tall, with blonde hair, blue eyes, and a beautiful smile. We introduced ourselves and asked her several questions. David knew just what to do to get her talking.

"Miss Cantone, first may I say you are beautiful," David said while shaking her hand. "We would like to see the files on all the cleaning crews." She seemed instantly attracted to David and would not let go of his hand. I was sure she fell in love with every handsome man she met, and I knew she would tell David anything he wanted to hear. She finally let go of David's hand, almost walking backward to get the files.

"Officer are you married?" she smiled.

"Does it matter?" David smiled back.

"Not to me, big boy," she purred as she came inches away from David's chest.

"Hey, big boy, give me that file," I growled. To my surprise, all it listed was "Bismarck Cleaning Service." Not one single name was listed, so I took down the address, and I showed it to the "big boy." We were both perplexed that there was no mention of any other places the crew had worked at. All this time, Miss Cantone would not stop talking, and I was getting a headache. I nudged David, and he asked her a question.

"Miss Cantone, have you ever met the cleaning crew?" he asked, looking into her eyes.

"Oh, yes, they are so nice, and real cute too. In fact, most late afternoons I open the bank doors and let them in. "Well, only on the days that the security team must leave early," she replied.

"So, who stays to let them out after they are finished?" David asked.

"I do. Then I set the alarm and go home."

"Miss Cantone, what are their names?" David asked, still flirting with her.

"There's Manuel Acosta, but I call him Manny, and his brother, Mateo Acosta," she replied as she twirled her hair around her finger.

"Where are they from?" David asked.

"Portugal, the Azores," she said and smiled at my "big boy."

"Now, Miss Cantone, you are so pretty; I'll bet you really like one of those men." David smiled.

"I will tell you, but you can't tell my boss." she laughed.

"I would never do that; in fact, I am jealous." David frowned.

"I am crazy about Manny," she whispered. She put her hands over her heart. "But now that I have met you, officer, I might be willing to stop seeing Manny." She sidled up close to David again. It was like I wasn't even in the room.

"Miss Cantone, would you know where they live?" David asked.

"Oh, yes, my handsome man," Miss Cantone replied. I gave David a disgusted look, but he squared his shoulders and went on.

"So, what is their address?" David asked, leaning in to Miss Cantone.

"Do you know Momma's Corner Store?" she asked.

"Yes, I have been in there before," David smiled.

"You have a wonderful smile, officer," she said breathlessly.

"Well, thank you. So, what about Momma's?" David asked.

"They live above the store," she said, putting her hands on her hips.

"Can you describe the apartment?" I asked. She gave me a look that could kill and never answered me. David grabbed her two hands and smiled.

"Please tell me." David looked into her eyes.

"I will tell you. When you walk up the outside stairs into the side door, you enter the kitchen. Then you go down the hall, with a living room on your left. If you continue down the hall, there's a bathroom on the right, and then a bedroom on the right and a larger bedroom on the left." She smiled.

"Thank you for that information. Is there a back stairway?" David asked.

"No, but there is one of those metal things outside of Manny's bedroom." She took hold of David's left arm.

"A fire escape, I suppose. Miss Cantone, which one is Manny's bedroom?" David continued.

"Call me Susan, please, and I will call you David. Manny's bedroom is the one on the left." She squeezed David's arm. "Such big muscles," she said admiringly.

"Susan, do they still work at the bank?" David asked.

She smiled. "Yes, David, but they have a thirty-day vacation coming up, starting tomorrow, and they are going back to Portugal. Manny wants to marry me, but I told him I would think about it.

David, if you tell me not to, then I won't marry Manny." She squeezed his arm again.

"If I were you, I would marry him," I said.

"I wasn't asking you." She dropped David's arm and scowled.

"Come on, 'big boy,' we have to go," I said.

David thanked Miss Cantone, and we both thanked the bank manager as we left the bank.

I grabbed David's arm. "Such big muscles, 'big boy'," I scoffed as I gave him another dirty look.

"Well, If I hadn't played the part, she would never have given us so much information," David said with a chuckle.

"Come on, 'big boy', let's get Tender and get to headquarters." I smiled and held his arm all the way there, rubbing his arm and telling him how much I loved his muscles. He never spoke a word all the way to headquarters.

Once there, we went and met with Chief Purdy. He was so happy we might have found the suspects that he thanked Tender. "We will follow up on this lead. Meanwhile, David, the FBI contacted me. They have a new case they want you to investigate. They are waiting for you at FBI headquarters."

EIGHT

FBI Director Lance

A few hours later, Tender, David, and I were at FBI headquarters. Tender had been invited to meet FBI Director Lance Steward. As we entered the building, Agent Sisson greeted us and bent over to whisper in Tender's ear.

"Thank you for saving my marriage. I am having a booze party this coming Saturday."

"I knew you would be okay." Tender smiled and gave him a high-five.

While we were being escorted through the building, Agent Sisson warned us that Director Lance, as he preferred to be called, didn't believe that a four-year-old could see things differently than trained agents. As we entered the room, Tender memorized her surroundings, as she always did.

"Good afternoon, Mr. and Mrs. Purdy and

Tender," Director Lance began. "Welcome to FBI headquarters."

"It's nice to meet you, sir. How can we help you?" I asked.

"Well, I wanted to meet the four-year-old who thinks she solved the case of the kidnapped boy."

Tender spoke up. "I know you don't believe in my abilities."

"No, I don't, I think it was a coincidence that you guessed correctly," Director Lance said as he crossed his arms over his chest.

"Well," Tender said, "Can I tell you something about you that I could never have known before?"

"Sure, give it a try," Director Lance said amiably.

"You just returned from Florida on a golfing trip. You golfed on ten different courses in five days. The only reason you came back was because of the missing boy. Nobody who works with you knew you were in Florida. You told everyone you were going to FBI headquarters in Washington. Instead, three agents from Washington who are your friends went with you, as they do every year."

Director Lance stood up. "How could you possibly know all that?"

"First, you have a nasty sunburn on the left side of your neck that would have taken five days to obtain, which means you are a right-handed golfer.

I said Florida, because the FBI has a retreat there for agents to get away and take a break."

"How did you know that?" Director Lance asked.

"I read a lot," said Tender and grinned at him.

"How much can a four-year-old read?" returned Director Lance.

"She has read over a hundred books so far this year alone," I chimed in.

"Last question: how did you know I went with agents from Washington DC?" Director Lance pressed.

Tender answered, "You did not want your agents to know where you go on your vacation, and no one golfs alone. Usually, golfers go in foursomes."

"Okay, fine; I am impressed." Then Director Lance added, "I asked you here for another reason. Agent Sisson is convinced you can help us on a case we need to solve quickly."

I asked if there was a reward, and he answered that there was a reward of $3,000. Tender tugged excitedly at my shirttail. "Okay, show me the evidence." she exclaimed.

Director Lance raised his hand in caution. "One more thing. Everything we do or say stays in this room."

The three of us promised to keep everything in confidence, and then Director Lance took us out to the hall and called for Agent Sisson. He told Agent Sisson to familiarize Tender with the "Bonnie and Clyde" bank robberies.

Once in the investigation room, Tender said, "Bonnie and Clyde?" That's cute. I guess it is a man and woman. But before we look at the "Bonnie and Clyde" case, we have a different case, the gorilla mask case, and we must act tonight."

Agent Sisson asked David to explain. Once all the information was given and Director Lance was informed, twenty-five agents were assembled, and Tender explained the plan.

"Over the past several years, two men from Portugal might have robbed many banks. They would work at the banks on the cleaning crew. They are brothers, and they are flying out tomorrow to go back to Portugal. Tonight is to be their last day of cleaning before they leave on a thirty-day vacation. They got away with over $9,865; from this robbery alone, as they only take what's in the teller's drawers. What I need is a couple of agents to be stationed in the bank as security guards. We will allow them to clean the bank and then go home, but we will follow them back home."

Just then, an agent raised his hand. "Why not arrest them in the bank?" he asked.

"What is your name?" Tender asked.

"Special Agent Robert Fleming," he responded.

"Thanks for your question, agent Fleming, but I believe the money is at the airport in a storage locker. Once they are in the airport, we can arrest them as they remove the money from the locker, and it is in their possession. Otherwise, we do not have enough evidence to convict," Tender replied. Then she sat down, as she was exhausted.

Agent Sisson took control of the room and gave orders to his men. He thanked us for all our help, and we headed home. As we walked out, he reminded us to report back tomorrow morning at 9 AM sharp to work on the "Bonnie and Clyde" case. We headed out, picked up pizza on the way home, and went to bed early.

The next morning was bright and sunny, and Tender was so excited she was in our bed early, shaking us awake.

"Tender, will you please let us sleep a little longer?" I groaned.

"Mom, I am hungry for the Eveready Diner pancakes," Tender said insistently.

Just then, David sat up. "Pancakes? Let's go!"

All Tender had to do was mentioned food, and David's stomach was awake. We all got showered and ready to leave. We ate at the diner and still arrived at FBI headquarters early. As we walked in,

Agent Sisson was entering the building at the same time. "Good morning, Purdys. You were correct; the brothers removed the money from an airport storage locker, and we recovered $56,500, which proves your theory that they robbed several banks." He shook his head and told Tender how amazing she was.

"Did anyone get hurt?" I asked.

"Nope. Everything went smoothly. Now please join me in the cafeteria for breakfast, on the FBI."

David yelled, "Breakfast sounds great!"

"David, you just finished a large breakfast. Isn't one breakfast enough?" I punched his arm.

"I am a growing boy." David protested. I gave him a kiss on the cheek, and Tender and I laughed all the way to the elevator.

We thanked Agent Sisson for the offer of breakfast, but we decided to head to the investigation room instead. Agent Sisson opened the elevator door with his pass. Then he headed to the cafeteria, and we headed to the seventh floor. When we got to the investigation room, several agents were already there, enjoying coffee and a muffin. Within thirty minutes everyone was present. Tender seemed quiet but confident, but I was overwhelmed with all the pictures and information on the walls. Tender focused on the map of the U.S. marked with the location where each bank robbery took place. Finally, she spoke up.

"Good morning, agents," Tender yelled. Every agent yelled back, "Good morning, Tender." Tender waved and said, "These robbers are not too smart. Mom, can you please get a pencil?"

One of the agents handed me a pencil. Tender directed me on how to draw what she requested. After we were finished, Tender turned around and asked, "What do you see?"

All the agents said simultaneously, "DK and CP." The robbers had picked locations that would spell out their initials on the map.

Next, Tender asked to see a blown-up picture of the robbers' right hands, which she examined with a magnifying glass, she noticed that DK and CP were wearing the same high school rings.

"They attended the same high school, which was within one hundred miles of their first robbery," she explained.

The agents began a search of every high school within a hundred-mile radius. There were forty-seven high schools. After one hour, they had narrowed down the search with both robbers' names: Derek Kline and Connie Padden. The next week, DK and CP were captured in Danville, Alabama, where they had been seen by the local police at a gas station.

Tender Answers the Call

Tender and David had opened a savings account and deposited the first reward in their new business account, Tender Purdy Inc., which she had earned for solving the case of the missing Russo boy. Now the account grew, adding her reward for solving the "Bonnie and Clyde" bank robberies case.

Tender loved solving cases, but as smart as she was, she had no concept of money.

NINE

Tender and the Mysterious Cold Case

On the way home from school, I told Tender about an unsolved case we had at our office. "Dad and I, along with every detective team, were given an unsolved case a little while ago. Now that you have solved that case for the FBI, we'd like to work on solving another unsolved case. Tender, we are having a problem reaching any conclusions on our case. But you should know that there is no reward."

"That's okay, Mom. I will try to help you solve it," Tender said. She was anxious to get started.

After dinner, when we gave Tender the file, David said, "Tender, we withheld some of the pictures, because they are too graphic for a four-year-old."

Tender told him that she needed all the information. "Besides, when I read your criminal justice books there were plenty of graphic pictures," she said.

David glanced at me, nodded, and gave her the complete file.

I said, "Okay, Tender, first question. Was this man murdered, or did he die of a heart attack?"

"I need one more piece of information," she replied. "I need to visit Angel Rodrigues's personal physician."

"Why is that important?" I asked.

"It is unlikely that a forty-two-year-old man would be on heart medication and die of a heart attack. But there might be a family history of heart disease," she said.

We arranged with our office to obtain a warrant to review all the medical records of Dr. Charles Benson. When we arrived at his office, he was more than willing to show us how healthy Angel Rodrigues was at his last exam, which was three months ago.

Tender reviewed the report. "His blood was clean. His heartbeat was perfect, at 56 beats per minute," she commented.

I asked Tender, "Is that good?"

"Athletes have a slower heartbeat, Mom," she replied.

"Young lady, how did you know that?" Dr. Benson stared at her in astonishment.

"I read a lot of medical journals," Tender explained.

"Just how old are you?" Dr. Benson demanded.

"I am four years old," Tender answered.

"And you read medical journals?" Dr. Benson asked, amazed.

"Yes," Tender confirmed.

Then Tender tapped her finger on the list of the victim's supplements. "Is it possible to inject mercury into any of these capsules?"

"Yes, most likely in the zinc. I suppose it could be injected," the doctor said thoughtfully.

Tender thanked the doctor, and we left with all the medical information, heading back to the police station.

At the station, we located the evidence box and checked it out. Tender took out the zinc capsules. "Dad, can you get me a magnifying glass?"

David brought one over, and we discovered that there was indeed a small pinhole in all the zinc capsules.

"This proves Angel was probably murdered," Tender said. "Now we need to test these zinc capsules to see if mercury has been added to them."

It took a few days for the lab to return the test results. I looked at the report and told David that after school, we should bring Tender back to the station and discuss the next steps with her.

Tender Answers the Call

After school, Tender was very excited and told me that she had a feeling she knew who did it. She reviewed the amount of mercury in the capsules and did some math. With this information, Tender determined how long it would have taken to kill Angel Rodrigues.

"Mom and Dad, based on the amount of mercury, it took forty-two days," she informed us.

We looked at the list of suspects who had been questioned, but we knew it would be difficult to locate all of them since this cold case was four years old.

The first individual we went to was the detective who had investigated the case. His name was Brandon Hanson. He was now with the North Dakota State Police. We went to see him early the next day.

Trooper Hanson was happy to meet the famous Tender Purdy, and he asked how he could help. Trooper Hanson was over six feet tall, with very broad shoulders, just like David. I noticed that he smiled all the time, even while speaking. I remember being taught in our state police training that we should always present a happy face.

Tender spoke up. "You were the detective handling the Angel Rodrigues case? What tests did you order?"

"I never thought that young man in good health

had died of a heart attack. I ordered a complete autopsy. Blood, kidney, and heart tests. Everything I could think of...Wait. Are you saying Mr. Rodrigues was murdered?" Hanson cried.

"Yes, by mercury poisoning," Tender informed him.

"I knew it!" he exclaimed. "Dr. Jason Fillmore was the doctor who performed the autopsy. He must have lied about what he found. Thank you. Please let me know who killed Mr. Rodrigues. I would like to be the one to inform the Rodrigues family who it was."

"We will let you know first," I promised.

After we left, I talked with Tender about why Dr. Fillmore would lie about his report. "I guess he knew something that would cause him some trouble," I mused. Tender agreed with me.

Next, we wanted to interview Mrs. Rodrigues, Angel's widow. She agreed that we could come over after she got off work the following day. Tender was excited. She informed us that she suspected Mrs. Rodrigues's husband had not been a U.S. citizen.

As we entered the Rodrigues house, we were surprised to see how beautiful their large home was. It was a center-hall colonial, with a beautiful oak spiral staircase that was visible as we entered.

Tender Answers the Call

The living room was magnificent, with a coffered ceiling and wainscoting on the walls.

A maid came in and asked if we wanted something to drink. Tender asked for a glass of juice; David and I asked for coffee.

Mrs. Rodrigues's brother-in-law, Victor Silva, was there when we arrived, but he was leaving as we came in. He shot us an angry look on his way out.

I informed Mrs. Rodrigues that we were investigating her husband's death. She was happy that someone was looking into it again and agreed to cooperate. Tender asked her what her husband had done for a living.

"Well, that is a little complicated. Talking with you could get me in trouble," she said nervously. I could see her hands were shaking and her breath was becoming more rapid and shallow.

"How old are you, young lady? How is it you are asking me these questions?" she asked.

"Mrs. Rodrigues, please don't be concerned about my daughter's age. She has this wonderful ability to solve difficult cases for the Bismarck Police. Now, are you able to answer her questions?" I asked.

"I am, as long as it gives me some answers about what happened to my husband," she replied, her voice shaking.

"Mom, can you and Dad go outside for a few minutes?" Tender requested. I gave her a questioning look, but we did as she asked.

"Mrs. Rodrigues, you have my promise that I will not speak a word about your secret," Tender assured her.

"How can, I be sure?" she asked.

Tender promised not to share anything told to her in private. Reluctantly, Mrs. Rodrigues then informed Tender that she and Angel were in the country illegally.

"We paid to get two Social Security numbers under our real names. We were told they came from young people who had never worked and had passed away," Mrs. Rodrigues said.

"Now tell me what your husband did for a living," Tender requested. "I know that you told the original detective he was an auto mechanic. I saw that in the report, but I knew that was impossible when I saw the picture of his fingernails. They were too clean."

"My husband was a famous private detective, and he went under the name of Zorro." Mrs. Rodrigues revealed.

"Yes, I have heard of him." Tender replied. "And you found a bank that would accept deposits under the name Zorro?"

"Yes, Zorro, Inc. Angel and I were the only

ones who could deposit or withdraw money," Mrs. Rodrigues confirmed.

"Is that how you came to have such a beautiful estate?" Tender looked around the room.

"Yes," said Mrs. Rodrigues, "Thank you for helping on this case. I will release you from your promise, Tender. I give you permission to reveal everything we just spoke about except for the fact that I am here illegally."

"Thank you, Mrs. Rodrigues. With your help, we can find the person who murdered Angel. I will need to report my findings to the police today," Tender said.

Mrs. Rodrigues gasped, "Murdered. I knew it." She started to cry. I went running in to see what all the commotion was about.

After making sure that everything was okay, I went over to Mrs. Rodrigues and hugged her. "I am so sorry about the loss of your husband," I told her.

A short time later, as we were leaving, Mrs. Rodrigues thanked Tender and called after her, "Please find my husband's killer."

Tender looked back and waved. "We will," she said emphatically.

On the way home, I explained to Tender to never to make promises that she could solve a murder.

We don't always find the person or persons who commit horrendous crimes.

"Yes, I am sorry, Mom," Tender said softly. Then Tender explained all that she had discovered.

"Tender," I said, "there's something you aren't telling us. What is it?" When Tender said she could not tell me, I said, "You must. Mrs. Rodrigues might be involved in the crime."

"I am pretty sure she is not," Tender replied.

"Tender, you need to tell us right now," David said.

"I would if I could, but I promised," said Tender.

"What do you mean?" I asked.

"It has nothing to do with this case. There is nothing that she has told me that would result in a sin against God," Tender said stubbornly.

"David, if Tender says she made a promise, and it has nothing to do with this case, I think we should believe her," I said after some thought.

"All right, I believe her; you know how it drives me nuts when I don't know everything," David grumbled. We all laughed.

"But Tender," I continued, "I don't want you making promises like this without checking with us first. After all, we are your mom and dad. Our job is to protect you." Tender nodded at me seriously, her eyes wide.

Once home, we started to get dinner ready: steak, mashed potatoes, and corn, David's favorite meal. Tender was trying to like it, but steak was hard for her to chew.

After dinner, we all went into the living room to discuss the case. I spoke up first. I brought up the autopsy that Dr. Fillmore did. "Tender, I think he was involved, but we don't know why he would want to kill anyone. Tomorrow I would check his bank account to see if anyone made a large deposit."

"Dad, you need to check out which one of the Rodrigues family members had the same amount removed from their account," commented Tender.

It took almost a week to discover who needed to be interviewed about the payment. David reminded us that there should be a warrant put out for Dr. Fillmore's arrest. Later he got the warrant himself and arrested him at the end of his shift.

Before the interview with the doctor, Tender spoke to David and me. "I have some bad news. Please put out a warrant for the brother-in-law, Victor Silva. Then have Mrs. Rodrigues brought in for questioning."

"Tender, you are not saying she had something to do with this, are you?" I asked.

"I don't know for sure, but I noticed something

in the house." Tender said. "There was a pipe on the mantel, and I could smell a cherry tobacco odor."

"I love that smell; it reminds me of when Father Gentry did daily Mass at St. Paul's, when I was in the orphanage. I could smell that on his clothes," I said.

"Honey, does that mean you two want me start smoking a pipe with cherry tobacco?" David asked, teasing.

Tender and I both yelled, "No way!" I also punched him in the arm for good measure.

"Okay, okay. Only kidding." He threw his hands into the air in alarm. I smiled at him in apology.

Mrs. Rodrigues was willing to come to the station, and she was placed in interrogation room four. The doctor was placed in interrogation room two. Finally, the brother-in-law, Victor Silva, was brought into interrogation room six. We could see him pacing past the window, as the blinds were completely open. First, David and Tender went into question Dr. Fillmore. The doctor seemed very nervous, as he was tapping his leg up and down at a rapid pace and sweating.

David read him his rights and then asked him if he would like an attorney.

The doctor put his hand up and wiped his lips, which were wet from the sweat. "No, I have nothing to hide," he said in a shaky voice. "Why would you think that I had anything to do with the death of Mr. Rodrigues?"

His face was turning red. I went in and brought him some water; he drank it down in just a few seconds. Moving back into the observation room, I watched him through the glass. I could see he appeared guilty and was about to break.

Tender began her questioning. "First, you lied on your report," she said, holding up one finger.

"I didn't lie. I sometimes make a mistake," said the doctor. His forehead was beginning to glisten.

"Yes, sometimes mistakes happen. Let's review your mistakes," Tender said, holding up two fingers. "When a person dies of mercury poison, he has liver failure, kidney failure, discolored eyes, and the heart finally fails, but it will show signs of poisoning."

The doctor was sweating so hard now that it was dripping into his eyes. "I guess I missed a few things," he admitted.

"How did you miss the blood work showing mercury in it?" David asked.

"I had no need to perform a blood test, because it was a heart attack." The doctor paused, then said, "I want a lawyer. I am not saying another thing."

"All right, just listen," David replied. "We know Victor Silva hired you to help him cover up the death of Angel Rodrigues, and he supplied the mercury. You deposited five thousand dollars into your account around the same time Mr. Rodrigues died. We also know that Victor Silva withdrew an identical amount the same day you made your deposit." As David spoke, Tender counted off the points against the doctor on her fingers—one, two, three.

Turning to her father, she said, "Now let's go over and offer a deal to Victor Silva."

As we got up to leave, the doctor yelled, "Wait! What's the deal?"

David spoke up. "Are you saying you no longer want an attorney to represent you in this matter?"

"Yes, but I want something in writing," the doctor demanded. I had been in the observation room with District Attorney Emma Peters. She and I moved into the interrogation room with Dr. Fillmore, David, and Tender.

Dr. Fillmore already knew the district attorney, who began with the first count of conspiracy to commit murder. "We are offering, today only, ten years' jail time with three years off for good behavior."

"No. I do not want any jail time." Dr. Fillmore shouted.

Then I spoke up. "I know that I really have no say here, but I would not be happy unless he served time in jail."

"Now," said the district attorney, "I will make one final offer. You serve five years without time off, and five years parole. But if we go to trial, I will seek twenty years, with no time off."

The doctor put his hands on his face and started crying. "All right, I will take the deal."

I handed him a pad. "Write down everything that happened," I said.

Afterward, we moved to Victor Silva's room and explained that the doctor had confessed to his part in the crime.

"Mr. Silva, I noticed you smoke cherry pipe tobacco; is this correct?" said Tender.

Silva adamantly denied using it, causing Tender to request that he remove his shirt.

"What for?" he asked.

"Our lab will detect the brand of tobacco you use," Tender explained.

"Fine, so I smoke cherry tobacco," he admitted defiantly.

"We know that you were having an affair with Mrs. Rodrigues," said the district attorney. "We also suspect she convinced you to kill her husband. North Dakota still has the death penalty, but if you are willing to tell us the whole story, we will take the death penalty off the table," the D.A. offered.

"No. I would rather die. She had nothing to do

with it." he shouted. Then he collapsed back into his chair, covered his face with his hands, and groaned softly.

Tender replied, "I believe you."

Once outside, we all asked Tender why she believed him. "Because he regrets ever doing it," was her reply.

Then Tender said, "Let's go talk to Mrs. Rodrigues. Don't forget, we promised Trooper Hanson he could be the one to tell Mrs. Rodrigues what happened."

David made a call to Trooper Hanson, and he arrived forty-five minutes later. David informed him of what we had discovered. We all filed into the interrogation room, and she greeted Trooper Hanson with a nod.

"What is going on?" she asked, trembling. "I am so confused."

"Mrs. Rodrigues, I have some bad news that may shock you." Trooper Hanson began by explaining that we knew about the affair with Victor Silva. "Mrs. Rodrigues, your brother-in-law killed your husband."

Mrs. Rodrigues turned as white as a sheet. Then she went over to the garbage can and started throwing up. "Mrs. Rodrigues, what happened to make Victor Silva want to murder your husband?" Trooper Hanson asked.

"He wanted me to divorce my husband. I told him it was over, and that I was still in love with my husband and that I had made a mistake." She started to cry, saying, "It's my fault Angel is dead."

Trooper Hanson thanked us for closing his case for him. He gave us all a hug and left with a tear in his eye.

That was the first unsolved case to be solved in almost nine years. Chief Purdy wanted to have a meeting about that on Monday, August 3, but I informed him that it was Tender's fifth birthday, and we were taking the day off.

It was hard to believe how fast the years were flying by. Besides, the chief was coming to the party. We could talk then.

Monday came fast. Our little girl was now five years old. The family all brought presents: clothes and jigsaw puzzles. Tender loved her present from us—a Cave Astrolabe telescope. It had excellent optics, fancy mounts, and adjustable pedestal legs. We were hoping Tender would take more interest in astronomy, as it was the one of the few subjects we couldn't get her interested in, even after we took her camping. We wanted to honor her first mother's wishes.

Everyone enjoyed the food, cake, and ice cream. When the party started to wind down, Chief Purdy asked if the four of us could meet in private. We headed to our bedroom. Tender and I sat on the bed, and the men remained standing.

"Well, Purdys, what you just accomplished was amazing. As you know, we have over forty unsolved cases, and we would love to solve even just half of them. So, I am asking you to work on all these cases. You would be our task force cold case unit. With one exception—if we have an active case that we are having trouble solving, you will look them over and help solve them," said Chief Purdy.

"There's just one problem with this, Chief. Tender helps us solve the cases, but she receives no compensation," I said.

Tender spoke up. "Money is not important, but I could never solve the cases without my mom and dad."

"I have a solution to that problem. We are going to the city council to ask for a special task force unit to solve unsolved cases. We will ask for additional staff. Tender will be on your staff as a consultant and will be paid $3.00 per hour for every case she works on. However, she will not be considered on the force. You will also be given an office administrator at the same rate as others on the force. If there is a reward, Tender will receive it as a civilian. Finally, you will interview several candidates who have just passed the detective exam. You will have your choice of anyone you choose. So, what do you think?" The chief had laid out the plan very well for us to consider.

"We will discuss it and let you know in a few days," David said.

After the chief left, we decided to discuss his offer. "Tender, what do you think?" I asked.

"Mom, you and Dad need to decide, not me," Tender said.

A few days later, while enjoying breakfast, David and I asked Tender for her opinion on whether we should take the new position at work.

"Am I the tiebreaker?" Tender asked.

"No. We have already decided, and we are curious about your input," I said.

Tender looked at us both and said, "I know you both have agreed to accept the new position."

"How do you know that?" I asked.

"I see how devoted you are to solving cases, and how you hate it when you hit a roadblock," Tender said with a smile.

That morning, we visited the chief to let him know that we were interested in taking the new position. We also told him the only reason we could accept the position is that when all three of us put our heads together, we could hopefully close some of these forty unsolved cases.

The chief asked us to attend the council meeting when it was scheduled. They would be taking the final vote on the proposal for the cold case unit.

"I knew you would take the position," smiled Chief Purdy. "Here are all the case numbers; please pick one for now, until the council approves this new department." The chief was hopeful that we could solve some old cases.

Tender was excited about being part of the police department. David told her not to be too excited yet, because the council needed to be convinced that this department was necessary for the health, safety, and welfare of the city of Bismarck.

TEN

The Real Estate Murders

Meanwhile, the FBI had asked us to help with a case, and we received permission from Chief Purdy to assist. All three of us would be going to FBI headquarters the following day. Tender was excited because she liked Agent Sisson and looked forward to seeing him again.

Agent Sisson was waiting for us as we entered headquarters. "Good morning, Purdys." he exclaimed.

We all replied with a hearty "Good morning to you, sir." as we entered the elevator. When the elevator stopped on the seventh floor, we all followed Agent Sisson to the investigation room.

As we came in, Director Lance stood up. "Before you receive any information on the case, the FBI has something for you, Tender. On behalf of the

FBI, I present this award for this young lady." He handed her a wallet that said *Federal Bureau of Investigation* on the outside.

Tender opened the wallet, and then took a deep breath. Enclosed was an FBI identification card with her name, picture, and her FBI number on it.

"What does this mean?" I asked.

"This gives her the right to enter the building without an FBI escort, as long as she is accompanied by you or David. Her status is FBI consultant. She also has other privileges, such as free meals in the cafeteria. She will also be invited to all FBI private functions, such as the awards banquet at the yearly ball."

Tender thanked Director Lance, and then waved to the other agents in the room.

Then Agent Sisson started to explain their case. "Unlike your local police, the FBI requires that cases involving murders across several states must never be left unsolved."

Tender already knew that, and she could not help but study the board instead of listening.

"This case involves women real estate agents. They were all murdered in the same way," the agent continued. "The perpetrator always sets an appointment to view a property. That's when he would overtake his victim."

Tender Answers the Call

"We decided not to allow Tender to see the photos, although we have a box that includes every photo for you, David and Elaine. This way, you can explain what is in the photos and decide what's appropriate for her," interjected Director Lance.

"The real estate company—was it the same one, or several different ones?" Tender asked.

"It was the same, but you will see our report on the company. Please keep the name to yourselves and tell no one. You, David, and Elaine are not allowed to ever engage anyone in conversation about any case you receive from the FBI that is ongoing, unless they are working on your team. Do you understand?" Agent Sisson demanded. We all responded that we understood.

Once back home, Tender marked the map to show the locations of the killings in seventeen different states. The last one was in North Dakota. She noted that all the murders were only in state capitals.

"Now I need to see the photos." Tender demanded.

"No way, Tender." I yelled.

"Mom, cover up the bodies and let me see the rest of the photo. How can I solve this crime unless I view all the evidence?" Tender asked.

Reluctantly, I covered up the bodies from the chest down, and Tender immediately started to notice mistakes the assailant was making.

"Mom, do you or Dad notice two mistakes the assailant made?"

I was busy making lunch, but David noticed the rope was the same material in all the photos.

"Dad, you are correct about the rope. It is a very rare type, made only in the Philippines, but sold in California. It is a hemp rope, made from plants," Tender explained.

Tender frowned at the photo again. "Dad, did you notice anything else?"

When he shook his head no, Tender continued, "This type of knot is a Navy knot, called the bowline knot. Although others use this kind of knot, my guess is the killer is a Navy man. He most likely received a dishonorable discharge. Finally, from the way the knots are tied, I can tell that we are looking for a left-handed person," Tender proudly explained.

David called Agent Sisson and updated him on what Tender had deduced. Agent Sisson said he would get his team working on this new information right away. Tender kept looking for more clues and finally gave up, going to bed quite late.

About 2 AM, Tender was awakened by a noise in the kitchen. Tiptoeing down the hall, she cautiously peeked around the corner into the kitchen to see what had made the noise. David and I were in the kitchen, making a late-night snack and talking.

She wanted to know what we were doing. I looked at this small person who should be in bed. "We were having trouble sleeping, so we thought we'd go through the case again to see if we could find another clue, but we haven't found anything yet," I replied.

"I had some more ideas while I was falling asleep," said Tender, munching on a leftover piece of pizza. "This person was a real estate agent and was very successful. But whatever the problem was that got him a dishonorable discharge from the Navy it will most likely get him fired from his real estate job." Tender yawned and turned to go back to her room.

Early the next morning, David called Agent Sisson. "Dwayne, I am sure Tender has uncovered some more facts that will help solve the case." David went on to explain what Tender had concluded.

I decided to return Tender to school. Because she learned at her own pace, she was not required to attend the minimum number of days. Although Principal Adler was always curious about the cases that she was working on, when asked Tender would only say it looked like we had solved an important one.

A few days later, we were summoned to FBI headquarters again. David and I picked up Tender from school. This time, she got a kick out of showing her FBI credentials. She scanned her badge, which allowed the elevator to bring us to the seventh floor, the investigation floor.

As soon as we walked in, all the agents in the room started clapping and cheering. Agent Sisson and Director Lance announced, "We have apprehended a suspect, Charles Flanagan, who received a dishonorable discharge from the Navy for stabbing a fellow sailor. He spent two years in Portsmouth Naval Prison. Once released, he changed his name and paid to have someone create a new identity and Social Security number for him." Director Lance paused to read his notes. "The mistake he made is that—"

"Wait!" Tender raised her hand. "Please let me guess."

"Okay, but you will never guess how we found the mistake," Director Lance smiled.

"My guess is that you have a word unscrambler that was invented in 1962," Tender guessed. "And that is why you were able to discover his identity, right?" Tender smiled.

"Charles Flanagan." She closed her eyes and said, "His real name is Harns Angel."

David and I just looked at each other. We knew Tender's mind did not work like ours or theirs.

Agent Sisson looked at us. "That is amazing. How do you do that?"

"I just see it," Tender explained.

The agent continued, "Then we contacted all the local real estate boards and asked them if they had any agents who were currently suspended. We found his information in the Bronx-Manhattan North Association of Realtors. We immediately got a federal judge to give us a warrant on the file of Harns Angel. The records said that he inappropriately touched a female agent from another real estate company. She had reported what happened, and he was suspended for one year."

Tender raised her hand again and was told to go ahead. "I am pretty sure he enjoyed real estate because most agents are women. I suspect he was very good at selling real estate, he tried joining different boards in different states. The problem is that most real estate agents are required to join the National Association of Realtors, and he was branded within that association as a predator. So, every time he got a no, he murdered one of the women to punish that company.

"I would also like to tell you how you apprehended the suspect," Tender continued. This was her favorite part. She got another nod from Agent Sisson.

"You contacted the National Association of Realtors and advised them to warn companies that he was on his way. Based on his travel pattern, he was heading west. It didn't take long before you received a call from the National Board, reporting that he was in Boise, Idaho. They followed your instructions, telling him that he would have to take the real estate test for that state. You set up a mock test with only FBI agents in the local Boise Board of Realtors room. Once everyone was seated and tests were passed out, he looked down to pick up his pencil. He was grabbed from behind and they arrested him." Tender just grinned at everyone's astonished faces.

The agents in the room loved listening to Tender's explanations, as they all stood to applaud her.

"Thank you, Purdys. If it's all right with you, we have set up a question-and-answer session for our agents to learn more about your family," said Director Lance. "Please report to my office after your session."

We followed Director Lance to a large auditorium. At the front were three chairs and a small table for us to sit at. Agents were already filling in the seats.

One at a time, agents would raise their hands, and I would point at one of them to hear their question.

"How is it living with a genius?" one agent asked.

"It has its challenges. If I am angry at David, Tender can tell something is wrong. She then quotes a Bible verse, and we are always supposed to make up," I answered.

He responded, "She even knows the Bible?"

"Every word. We are so proud of her, because she does not like to disobey God," I answered proudly.

Almost every hand went up. I pointed at one of the female agents. "Tender, is it true you were adopted?"

"Yes, my mother was dying of cancer. I never knew who my birth father was. My first mom and I chose the Purdys, and then the Purdys chose me. I feel so blessed to have had two mothers and two fathers," Tender said.

"I thought you said you never knew your birth father," the agent responded.

"I never did, but I have my dad, David, and my Father God." Tender smiled. All the agents took a deep breath at the same time.

Agents kept asking questions as the session went on. Finally, one agent asked the last one. "Mr. Purdy do you regret adopting Tender?"

"That is a foolish question, but I will answer it anyway. I never knew I could love a child as much as I love my wife. Now I do, and I have two people to love. Why would I regret that?" David answered.

"So, who is better at solving mysteries, you or your wife?" the agent said with a smile.

"I refuse to answer on the grounds it might incriminate me," David grinned, and they all laughed.

The agents wanted to keep asking questions, but I told them that we were tired and hungry, and that Director Lance was still waiting for us to report to him.

We headed over to his office. "I do enjoy how you Purdys solve these cases so easily," Director Lance noted, then added, "Well, I have some good news. The National Association of Realtors has a reward leading to the arrest and conviction of the "Real Estate Killer." The reward is the largest ever paid out, $25,000."

It was a good thing we were all sitting down. David and I were in shock. My body went numb, and I could barely process Director Lance's next words. Tender, on the other hand, had no concept of money and just wanted to go home.

"I will need a few things from you. Tender will need a Social Security number," Director Lance said.

"We got one when she was adopted. It was a requirement," I said in a daze.

"Great. As soon as the reward arrives, I will contact you." He handed us a form requiring a saving account and filing with the state either as Tender Purdy, Inc., or as a North Dakota corporation. He did not know we had already done that.

But David asked about the corporation. He was leaning forward and looking at Director Lance intently, and I could tell he wanted to know if there was any benefit to being a corporation that we had not already discussed.

"We are not allowed to pay rewards to any police officer. Now that she is officially a consultant, we need to pay her company. She will receive a 1099 tax form every year. The first reward we paid her as a regular citizen," the director explained patiently.

"Finally, I would like to offer you and David a position here on my team at the FBI," Director Lance smiled. "Don't answer me now. Please take some time to consider my offer. As an added incentive to help you make your decision, we will double both of your salaries."

David and I were shocked as we looked at each other. As we left, David started to jump up and down. "We could be FBI agents, and the pay increase will be fabulous." he said excitedly.

"Calm down, David. We have a lot to consider. We may be required to relocate to another state or even out of the country. I will not have my daughter living anywhere but in Bismarck. She needs her family, her cousins, and her friends, whom she loves." I glared at David with my arms crossed.

"You are right, Elaine. I could never leave here. I love my life the way it is right now." David smiled at me, hoping I would smile back.

I jumped into his arms and gave him a big kiss.

"Elaine, at times you can be frightening," David said ruefully.

"I know. It is my motherly instinct to protect our daughter," I responded.

We held hands as we walked to the car. Then David said, "Elaine, it was pretty flattering to be invited to be agents."

"Yes, David," I replied, "but it was because of Tender we were even asked."

We both started to laugh, and he kissed me just as we reached the car.

"David, I love you," I said with a smile.

"Elaine, you make me so happy, and I love you too," David replied.

Of course, Tender had to get into the action, and we both told her how much we loved her and gave her a big hug.

ELEVEN

This Hits Home

As usual, once we got home, David went for the mail, hoping his fishing magazine had arrived. Tender and I just laughed as we heard him yell, "Yes!"

I headed to the kitchen to fix us a snack before dinner; we were planning to relax and watch some television. Mary was coming for dinner with her new boyfriend and David was going to pick them up.

"Honey, you have a letter from St. Paul's School for Girls," called David, as he brought in the mail. I asked him to bring it to me in the kitchen, which he did. Then he stood there staring at me.

"What?" I laughed.

"Aren't you going to open it?" he asked.

"Don't you have to pick up Mary and her new boyfriend?" I reminded him.

"All right, I'm going. But don't open it without me." he said.

Soon, David was back with Mary and her boyfriend. As they entered, Mary introduced us to her new boyfriend, Richard Harris. I gave him a hug and welcomed him into our home. Tender went over and greeted him too, but there were no hugs from her until she knew him better. Tender was standoffish to anyone she didn't know.

He shook her hand and said, "So this is the famous Tender Purdy I have heard so much about."

Tender smiled and replied, "I am not famous; I am only five years old."

"Okay, then, tell me something about me that no one else could possibly know." requested Richard. He crossed his arms over his chest and waited.

Mary and David held up their hands as if to warn him, and Mary teased, "I wouldn't do that if I were you."

"I am not afraid of anything she might say." responded Richard.

"First let me see your hands," requested Tender. After she examined his hands closely, she had him stand up and turn all the way around.

"Richard, you live alone with your dad. Your mom left within the last few months. You work at a market in the fish and meat department. Your last girlfriend broke up with you because you have had difficulty with the family breakup. Your grades are slipping, and Mary has been helping you with your class work. You have been starting to feel better over the last few weeks since you have been seeing Mary. If it wasn't for her, you were going to quit school and go into the military. Finally, you are very smart, but since Mary started helping you, you've been playing dumb." Tender didn't hold back.

Richard blushed bright red, and angry tears started in his eyes. He was about to leave when Mary and I sat him down. Richard took a few moments to get himself under control. I spoke first.

"Richard, we would love to know you better. Please, let's eat, and then we can talk."

Tender apologized and put her hand on Richard's arm. "Richard, I am sorry I upset you."

"No, don't be. I have been holding everything back and lying about my mother and father, so thank you for helping me tell the truth."

After our spaghetti and meatball dinner, we all went into the living room to relax.

Richard had been looking at Tender from the corner of his eye. Then he spoke up. "Tender, you are amazing. How did you know all that just from looking at my hands?"

"Richard, are you sure you want to know?"

"Yes, please."

"Okay, Richard. I noticed your clothes were wrinkled, which tells me there is no one doing enough laundry for you and your dad to look good."

"But how did you know it was only a few months ago that my mother left?" he asked.

"My best guess was that it would take a few more months before you learned how to do laundry and iron your clothes," Tender replied.

"I guess from the fish smell you knew I worked at a market. But I didn't have on my work clothes, and I took a shower after work," continued Richard.

"I have a very strong sense of smell, and your hands smelled of fish and raw meat," Tender said.

"And how did you know about my old girlfriend?" Richard asked.

"She still has your high school ring, which goes on your right hand. There is still a pale ring mark on your finger. She has not returned your ring yet because she might want to get back together with you, but you have very strong feelings for Mary," said Tender.

"Wait," Mary injected, "why do you think he has feelings for me?"

"Well, he was biting his fingernails after his family split up, but he stopped a few weeks ago. When did you start seeing each other?" Tender asked.

Tender Answers the Call

"A few weeks ago." said Mary with a grin.

"The oddest thing you mentioned was about me joining the military. How could you know that fact? I told no one." Richard pressed.

"You blame your father for the breakup, and because your father was in the military, you became desperate. You figured the military was your only option. But a few nights ago, you most likely heard your father asking forgiveness from your mom on the phone. I predict they are going to marriage counseling and will reunite in a few weeks," replied Tender.

Richard came over to Tender and gave her a hug. Tender put her arms straight down at her sides and looked at me, feeling uncomfortable. Tender let out a sigh of relief as he let go of her.

Richard looked at Mary. "I am not sure how you feel about me, but Tender is correct. I do have feelings for you."

Mary smiled and spoke as she turned and walked toward him. "Richard, I have had feelings for you since the fifth grade." We all looked at Tender and started laughing.

TWELVE

Sister Mary Ellen Needs Help

David had been sitting and watching the scene between Richard and Tender, and now he decided it was time to make his request.

"Elaine, before we watch a TV show, would you please read your letter?" He got it off the counter and handed it to me, as I read it out loud.

> *My dear Elaine, I am writing to you with tears in my eyes, as my heart is broken by what I am about to tell you. Four of my girls have gone missing in the last four months. You may remember them, as they were very young when you attended St. Paul's.*
>
> *It started four months ago, when the first girl went missing. Allie Smith came to us at birth. She was so cute; she had curly red hair, so curly*

we could do nothing with it. I remember many girls tried to comb it without making her cry. She always wanted you to comb it for her.

"I remember her; she was very polite, and about five or six years old. She was short for her age and was a very happy child. I really liked her. She was also like me; she had only a first name, and was given the last name Smith," I said thoughtfully. Then I continued:

Allie was fourteen years old when she went missing. The next girl was Vicky Smith, almost fifteen years old; she went missing just one month later. It is possible she ran away, as she was bitter. She came to us as a baby, but she gave us nothing but trouble.

"Vicky was one of the deaf children; when she came, we all had to learn sign language, and the teachers had to instruct us all in sign language. I liked her the most," I said sadly.

Richard asked a question. "Why not just have special classes for the deaf, like they do in our school?"

"The school, even though it was an orphanage, wanted to make sure the Deaf were part of the family. So, we always had to speak with our voice and sign," I replied.

"That's really nice, but also hard." replied Richard.

"As I was saying, she was bitter, but I believe she struggled in school and was frustrated. I tried to help her with her studies. She was very smart, but she could only muster up average grades at best. She was seven years old when I was about to leave," I continued.

Tender remained quiet, which was her method of studying a case. Richard seemed fascinated with detective work. Mary just shook her head; she was used to it by now. Hearing about mysteries was nothing new to her. However, she did find it interesting that Richard found it so fascinating.

"Let's move on," I said, continuing with the letter.

This one bothers me the most. Brittany Smith, fourteen years old; she was special, smart, loving, kind, and always a proper young lady. Why would such a child want to run away?

I thought back to memories of Brittany. "This girl was loved by every single person at St. Paul's. She was funny, and she made all of us laugh. She wouldn't have run away unless something was wrong," I said as I looked at Tender.

Tender Answers the Call

Tender remained quiet as I continued with the letter.

The last girl to go missing was Paula Smith, seventeen years old. Why would she go missing? She had been accepted at Bismarck State College for the free tuition program, just like you were. The only requirement is to serve in state or city public service.

I remembered that she also wanted to be in law enforcement. "She was nine years old at the time I left, and I remember her saying to me when I left, 'Hey, Elaine, see you on the police force someday.'"

Then I finished the letter from Sister Mary Ellen.

Please find my girls, whom I love. You know how to find me. I love you very much. May God be with you.
Sister Mary Ellen

Tender asked to see the letter. As I handed it to her, Richard came over to see it too. Tender took several minutes to study the contents, and then she asked Richard, "What do you see?"

He replied, "I don't know what you mean."

"What does the letter tell you?" Tender retorted as she looked back at him.

"Well, it tells me about four girls who are in trouble," replied Richard.

"Yes, but look deeper into the letter," pressed Tender.

"I don't see anything else. Sorry." Richard exclaimed in frustration. He ran his hand through his hair and let out an exasperated sigh.

"Do you notice the discoloration in the paper?" Tender asked.

"Yes, are those her tears?" asked Richard.

"Yes, but you need to see the whole picture. This beautiful person is crying from the top of the letter to the bottom, in total pain over losing four of her children. When you are given a child to care for from birth, and they become your very own, then you cannot lose them without hurting inside," Tender said quietly.

"Tender, that is amazing. I love this—it is so interesting." Richard said excitedly.

Then Mary spoke up. "Calm down, cowboy! Time for a movie."

Everyone laughed at Mary's words as David made popcorn. Every Saturday night we usually played a game and watched a movie. Lately, Mary had brought a different date each time. Tender liked Richard: he was nice, and she thought Mary liked him too. But one thing she had learned about love was that she was not very good at figuring out who Mary really liked. Tender had thought she liked the last three boys, but she was wrong all three times. I kept telling her that it was not easy to find the evidence in the case of Aunt Mary's love life.

After the movie, David was about to take Mary and Richard home, when Tender asked, "Mary, is he the one?" Mary only smiled and said, "We will see, Tender." That's what she always said, and I, having supermom hearing, would just laugh.

On his way out, Richard said goodbye and asked Tender to keep him informed about our case.

"As you wish, Detective Richard Harris," was her reply.

As we all went to bed, I told Tender that we could discuss the case tomorrow, after church.

Tender woke up early every Sunday because it was her favorite day of the week. We would head to the Eveready Diner for breakfast, and then go to church. The message this Sunday was about Jonah and the big fish. Tender had stopped bringing her Bible to church as of last year. She had memorized almost all of it except the Book of Revelation, written by the apostle John. I had forbidden her to study it until she got older.

After church, we headed to Alex and Loriann's house. Tender would play with her cousin Anne all day. To my surprise, Richard Harris arrived to meet the rest of the family. This was the first boy David's sister had ever dared bring to the family gathering. Richard was introduced to Jake and Louise Purdy, David and Mary's dad and mom.

"Hello, young man. So, you think you would like to keep seeing my daughter?" asked Jake as he put his strong hand on Richard's right shoulder and squeezed it tight.

"Yes, sir," Richard said in a squeaky voice, and his knees started to buckle. Mary had warned him about her dad, but Richard was still surprised. Everyone else laughed. Mary was watching nervously from the other room. She knew that if anyone could scare off a suitor, it was her dad.

"Okay, son, I am going to give you a test." stated Grandpa. Mary and I just looked at each other, then at Richard. His eyes were wide open in fear.

Also observing this scene, Tender whispered to her cousin Anne, "Without a doubt, he is going to need our help."

Grandpa led him into the puzzle room. "All right, son; in order to earn a meal around here, you have to complete at least one quarter of this puzzle, understand?"

"Yes, sir," Richard replied, still in a squeaky voice.

Grandpa asked Richard, "Is that how you talk all the time?" Richard gave him a weak smile.

As soon as Grandpa left the room, Mary entered. "Richard, are you okay?"

"I guess you did warn me he would have a task for me to prove myself, but a jigsaw puzzle?"

Just then, Anne and Tender walked in. Mary looked at them and smiled. "Richard, let's just sit down and let the girls do their thing."

Anne and Tender started placing pieces at an amazing rate. Richard was so amazed that he stood up to watch. They completed the puzzle in forty-five minutes. Richard put his hands on his head and just laughed.

"How is that possible? A thousand-piece puzzle in forty-five minutes!" Richard just shook his head back and forth with his hands on his hips.

"Tender and I are the fastest puzzle solvers in the family, and we have done this particular puzzle, the forest butterfly, before," explained Anne.

Richard looked at Tender and Anne. "I think I love you girls."

Tender replied, "The questions is, do you love Aunt Mary?" He just chuckled but did not answer.

Tender looked at her aunt and whispered, "He does."

Mary blushed and looked thoughtful. When

Richard asked what Tender had said, Mary said, "Never mind. Just leave the room a few minutes after we go. Remember, you cannot lie to my father. He is going to demand you tell him who really completed this puzzle. Just smile and shrug your shoulders, and everyone, including my dad, will laugh."

Richard walked out of the room strutting like a peacock, thrusting his shoulders back and forth as he entered the dining room. Mary just put her hands over her face; she knew her dad hated strutting.

As Richard sat down between Mary and me at the kitchen table, Jake exclaimed, "Young man, I told you not to come out until you finished one quarter of that puzzle, and that should take hours."

He went into the puzzle room and yelled, "No way! Young man, if you think I don't know what is going on here, you are mistaken. There are only two very small persons, whom I will not mention by name, who can complete a thousand-piece puzzle in less than an hour."

Richard said nothing; he just shrugged his shoulders, lifted his hands into the air, and opened his eyes wide in mock amazement.

Grandpa gave Richard a dirty look, and then he laughed. He shouted, "Smart move, young man. That's what I would have done." Everyone burst out laughing except Richard. Those who had food in their mouths choked and spluttered. Mary just looked at Richard, who was sweating, and grabbed his hand under the table.

Before leaving, Richard and Mary came up to us, and Mary asked. "Have you decided what you are going to do about the St. Paul's mystery?"

"Not yet. We are heading home to sit at the kitchen table and discuss our theories," I replied.

"Can we come along?" asked Richard with a big smile.

"Sure!" shouted Tender. David and I just looked at each other and sighed. We all got into David's Mercedes, our Sunday-only car. We used my Chevy Chevelle Super Sport for everyday driving. I never let David drive my car, but I drove his Mercedes all the time. Tender thinks it is because her dad is smart when it comes to me. He hardly ever says a word when we are discussing a case. He would rather listen and observe Tender and me in action. He always says it is like magic how the two of us think alike.

Once we were home, David told everyone to go to the investigation room. We had converted the spare bedroom into an investigation room after Tender's first case. It had a long, narrow table with eight chairs. In front of each chair was a pad and pencil.

Richard took a deep breath as he chose his seat next to Mary. Mary said, "Calm down, Richard, or you might explode." He just shook his head back and forth.

I always ran the chalkboard, as David was not very good at spelling. "We have one rule: no interrupting when someone is giving input," I reminded everyone.

"Okay, what do we have so far?" Richard asked.

I turned the question back on them. "Richard and Mary, what do you see so far?"

Mary went first. "I see four different girls with different circumstances."

"Correct, but what do they all have in common, Richard?" I pressed.

Richard sat up tall and looked at Mary, who said, "Don't look at me."

"Well, they are all orphans from St. Paul's," Richard said.

Mary jumped back in. "They all went missing in the first week of four different months."

Tender was happy to see Mary involved, as she usually had no interest in our cases. She must have wanted to impress Richard.

Tender said quietly, "They all have the last name of Smith."

I jumped in too. "They all seemed happy at the orphanage, except for Vicky Smith, the deaf girl."

Richard raised his hand and waved it back and forth.

"Richard, you don't need to raise your hand; just go ahead and say what you're thinking," I told him.

"I think since they all went missing during the first week of different months, then they were all somehow tricked." Richard blurted out.

Tender smiled. "Very good, Richard! Let's look at his theory."

Everyone was taking notes on what they had uncovered so far. Mary added on, pointing at Richard, "It has to have been someone who is working inside the orphanage."

I chimed in. "Yes, but they would only be working the first week in any given month."

Tender looked happily at her mom, as if to say, "This is going well."

"That is correct," said Tender out loud. "We are looking for that person (or persons) who delivers only once a month, in the first week of the month." She looked at me expectantly.

I was having trouble putting all my thoughts together; it had been a long time since I had been at St. Paul's. Suddenly I shouted, "The food service company. What was their name?" I was drawing a blank.

Tender told me what she does when she needs

to recall something hidden in her brain. "Mom, close your eyes; visualize the truck, and you will remember their name."

I closed my eyes for a few minutes. Then, out of nowhere, I saw the truck in my mind. "I've got it. 'Apples and peaches fresh from our farm' was on the side of their truck." I started to dance around the room, throwing my arms into the air. We all laughed because Richard started doing the same thing.

"Richard Harris, this isn't *American Bandstand*. Sit down," Mary yelled.

"Yes, I remember now. Lincoln Farms," I smiled as I sat back down. "Tender, can you share with us what you are thinking?"

"Okay, Mom, I remember you told me that while you were at St. Paul's, you had no contact with any boys or family at all. It would be easy to have these girls think a boy had been watching them from a distance and was in love with them, or that their parents had been looking for them and had found them. Mom, if you were told someone knew who your parents were and that they were looking for you, what would your reaction be?" Tender asked.

"I could have been convinced to run away and be with my family. I dreamed for almost eighteen years that someday I would be reunited with any family I had," I said sadly.

Richard jumped in. "So, if it was a boy would it be the same boy for all the girls?"

"Yes, and then the scam begins," Mary spoke up. "But I would not leave just because a boy said he loved me. I bet the story was that the family is looking for their missing daughter who was kidnapped. And they have never stopped looking for her."

"I'm sure you're right. I suppose the kidnapper told them he knew who their parents or grandparents were," I agreed.

"Is that enough of a reason?" Mary asked.

"Yes. If someone said, 'Your family has been trying to find you, and they hired me. I only work on this crew as a front to locate you.' Then they would warn the girl, 'Tell no one, not even your best friend, or you will never see your family.' The girl would then follow their instructions about the day and time and where they would be waiting," I concluded.

David jumped in. "That's it. Looks like we have a case." David always had the last word.

Richard asked, "What's next?"

"First, we need to present our case to the Bismarck police chief. Then, with his approval, we go to the FBI, because all kidnapping cases go there," I said.

Mary was starting to enjoy this mystery. "What if you get a no from everyone?"

Tender banged her fist on the table. "Then the fun starts because the bad guys don't stand a chance against the Purdy team. Right, Dad?"

"Right." he responded.

I suggested we call it a night because David had to take Mary and Richard home. As we all said good night, Richard said, "I love this kind of work, and someday I might want to be on the Purdy team." Everyone laughed except Mary, who just shook her head.

Tender was excited about the new case for reasons unknown even to David and me. The week before, she had received a private letter from her benefactor, which revealed a secret she needed to keep to herself. She received several such letters a year. Tender always followed the Bible text in Matthew 9:30: "And their eyes were opened. And Jesus sternly warned them, 'See that no one knows about it.'" Tender never did reveal any secret told to her unless she felt comfortable that Jesus would approve.

The next morning, I was tired from being up late. I couldn't get Sister Mary Ellen's tears out of my mind, and I'd had trouble sleeping. So, we all headed for breakfast at the Eveready Diner for the second day in a row. Everybody was happy to see Tender. Her favorite waitress, Lillian was always trying to trick her up with a Bible question.

"Tender," she asked, "there were ten brothers who did not like their younger brother, so they threw him into a pit. Who was he?"

"Lillian, the man was Joseph," Tender replied easily.

"Tender, one of these days I will trick you up." laughed Lillian.

"Lillian, I am sure you will someday." Tender replied.

After breakfast, we arrived at the police station for our meeting with Chief Purdy. I explained the case we had discovered. "Elaine, I will contact the Lincoln chief of police and get back to you by tomorrow," he said.

We thanked Chief Purdy and decided to let Tender hang out with us for the day. She spent most of the day visiting with all her detective friends and helping them fill in some missing pieces in their cases. At one point, David got upset at Detective Jimmy Johnson. When Tender gave him enough information to solve his case, he uttered a bad word. He looked over at David. "Whoops, sorry, Tender. I didn't mean to say that. It just slipped out."

David gave him a dirty look. Several of the

detectives yelled, "Hey, Jimmy, be careful in front of our girl." Then Tender yelled, "Someone get the rope." Everyone laughed.

I decided it was time for lunch, so a bunch of us went to the cafeteria. Tender sure could gather a crowd. Every officer wanted to sit near her. She knew everyone by name, even if she had been introduced to them only once. She would always ask questions about their family as if they were old friends. One of Tender's favorite people was Detective Leon Foster, who had been on the force for thirty years.

Once back upstairs after lunch, Chief Purdy said, "I have an answer from the Lincoln Police Department." We followed him back to his office, and he shut the door behind us. "Chief Beck feels these girls are just runaways and has denied you from entering his jurisdiction."

"Why?" Tender asked.

"Well, there's some history between us, and we don't see eye to eye on some police procedures that were voted on in the past. I was the deciding vote. He disagreed with me, and ever since then, we get very little cooperation from his department."

"Would it do any good if I went and pled our case with him?" I asked.

"You could try" he replied. "But you might have

better luck with FBI Agent Tender Purdy requesting them to open a new case."

"Won't that embarrass him, once we solve this case in his jurisdiction?" David asked.

"Yes, but he is the youngest chief in the state, and he could use a little humility," remarked Chief Purdy drily.

"Let's give him a second chance before we go over his head to the FBI," I suggested.

The next morning, we all headed to Lincoln, North Dakota, a three-hour ride away, to meet Chief Allen Beck.

As Chief Purdy had suspected, Beck was insulted that we would dare approach him after he said no to opening a case for what he thought was a bunch of runaways. So, David pursued the only other option, which was to contact Agent Sisson.

"Tender requests a meeting with you as soon as possible," said David, on the phone with Agent Sisson. The agent said he could see us on the following day.

"Tender, are you getting hungry?" I interrupted.

"Yes, Mom, we children are very hungry!" David said. Tender and I started laughing.

"Okay, how about bringing home pizza from Ashley's Pizzeria?" I suggested.

David and Tender agreed, then Tender said,

"Mom, get an extra-large with half pepperoni and half veggie too."

"Why would I do that?" I asked.

"Well, you don't want Richard and Mary to watch us eat, and not have anything to offer them, do you?" Tender chuckled.

"You think they are at our house right now?" David asked.

"Dad, they have been there since school got out," grinned Tender.

As we rounded the corner and our house came into view, there they were, waiting for us on the porch. They both stood up and waved.

"How did it go today? Do we have a case to solve?" asked Richard.

"Let's eat first, and then we can talk about the case," I said quickly.

"We can just make something from here," Mary said , not seeing the pizza.

"No need." Tender called after her. "I knew you were here, so we got you both your favorite."

Mary yelled back, "Thank you so much."

Once Mary came to the table, we thanked God for the food and Tender announced that she needed to say something. "Mom, Dad, I think it's obvious, don't you?"

"David, don't you hate Tender's obvious solutions, which we never know?" I teased.

"Dad, it is so obvious we need to get Mary a house key. We can't have our loved ones sitting outside for hours."

"Well, that could cause a problem with my dad," David hesitated.

"I was not suggesting they be in the house alone, but rather on the porch. But if they had a key, they wouldn't have to wait to use the bathroom, like Mary just did. She could get them drinks or a snack, while Richard remained outside."

"I could live with that," David agreed.

"Mary, I will give you my key, and I'll make a new one for myself tomorrow," I said.

After we finished eating, I explained how the Lincoln chief denied our request to open a new case, since he thought it was just a few runaways. "We have requested a meeting with our FBI contact, Agent Sisson. He should contact us in the morning with a meeting time."

"Hmm, okay. So, what else do we know about the girls?" asked Richard.

"Nothing, until we meet with Sister Mary Ellen," I replied.

"Well, when are we going to St. Paul's?" replied Richard.

"Most likely in the next few days, while you are in school," David said.

"Fine, but I don't understand why Tender can skip school and we can't," Richard said, disappointed. He slumped back in his chair.

"Richard, Tender doesn't get behind in school or worry about exams like we do," replied Mary.

"Mary, are you going to break up with Richard?" Tender asked.

"What? Are you breaking up with me?" said Richard, jumping up in a panic.

"No, I am not breaking up with you." Mary glared at Tender.

"Okay, then you do love him, don't you, Mary?" Tender said.

Richard looked questioningly at Mary. "I hope you do, because I am falling in love with you, Mary," he said shyly.

"Richard, I do love you," replied Mary with a blush.

Just when they were about to kiss, David put his hands in between their mouths. Everyone laughed.

"Well, it is not official until Richard gets that ring back from what's-her-name," Tender announced.

"Yes, Lila Miller," Mary said, grimacing.

The next morning, I took Tender to school and told Mrs. Adler that we had a new case. Of course, she wanted me to fill her in.

"I wish I could, but we are not allowed to discuss

the case openly," I replied. I let her know that if we get a call from the FBI, I will have to pick up Tender. Mrs. Adler was excited for Tender, and she knew once the case was solved, Tender would fill her in about how she solved another mystery.

In the meantime, David and I headed to police headquarters and were given another unsolved case.

"I am giving you one of our oldest unsolved cases. I will not be disappointed if your team is unable to solve this one. Remember, always work on hot cases when they arrive," said Chief Purdy.

I took the envelope from the file and started to review the case when a call came in from Agent Sisson. So, off we went to get Tender.

When we arrived at FBI headquarters, Tender made a new friend right away.

"Tender Purdy, please come over to the front desk and sign in. Good morning. My name is John Riley, but my friends call me Big John," came a big, booming voice.

When we walked over to the front desk, we were met by a large black man. "Big John, how tall are you?" asked Tender curiously.

"I am 6 foot, 4 inches tall, and I am a solid 280 pounds of muscle," Big John said with a chuckle.

Tender asked, "Can I guess some things about

you without you telling me?" Her eyes were quickly going over him and his desk, picking up details.

"Sure, give it a try," he replied. He leaned over his desk to look down at her.

"You were one of the top agents in the FBI until you were shot in the leg, so now you have restricted duty....How am I doing?"

"So far, pretty good," smiled Big John.

"You had an amazing wife, whom you met in college, and you celebrated twenty-five years together, but she passed away right after you returned from a thirty-day vacation in Hawaii, three years ago. You stayed at the FBI retreat on the mainland.

"You have three girls. The oldest are twins and are married. The youngest just graduated college and is very special to you, since she is in FBI training as we speak. She wants to be like her daddy, an FBI agent."

"That's amazing, Tender. How could you know all that?" Big John boomed.

"Well, when I was touring the building, I saw a picture of your family when you were receiving an award. Your wife was not in the picture, but your kids were. It was obvious the oldest are identical twins, and the youngest was looking up at you like she wanted to follow in your footsteps. The plaque also has the date you started with the FBI.

"On your desk, you have a picture of you and your wife on your wedding day, and it has the date on it. About Hawaii: the FBI offers agents who have faithfully served for twenty-five years, their choice of FBI retreats and Hawaii is the most beautiful location. So, after you offered your beautiful wife her choice, it was a no-brainer. I also noticed that on the plaque, every family member was named, but your wife was not," she said. "I am so sorry for your loss, but because of your girls, you are doing fine." Tender and Big John both had tears in their eyes.

"Big John, can I ask you a personal question?" Tender asked.

"Yes, but be careful." Big John replied. He straightened up in his chair.

"Can we be best friends?" Tender smiled.

"I would love that, Agent Tender Purdy. That was amazing. I think I love you." Big John laughed loudly and slapped his knee. Tender grinned happily.

"All right, you sign here, and register your parents down here as guests, and now you get a lollipop from Big John," said Big John.

"Do I get one?" asked David, eyeing the jar of lollipops longingly.

"Sorry, agents only," replied Big John. He glared at David.

As we headed upstairs, Tender thanked Big John for her rainbow lollipop.

"Tender, I have never seen a lollipop so big, and with so many colors, like in a rainbow," David drooled.

"Dad, would you like a lick?" Tender offered, holding out the pop.

"I thought you would never ask! Thanks, dear." He took a few licks. "Wow, that is good. If it is the last thing I do, I will trick Agent Riley into giving your dear old dad a rainbow pop," David vowed.

Once we were upstairs, all of Tender's agent friends came over to say hello. Then Agent Sisson instructed us to follow him. We went into Director Lance's office.

"Good morning, Team Purdy. I have received the files on all the runaways from Chief Beck. He refused cooperation, saying it was a wild goose chase. I got my hands on it by contacting State Police Colonel Stoney. He has jurisdiction over every police chief in North Dakota. I was surprised Beck denied me; he must think he has the final say in his jurisdiction. But he is young, and in time he will learn how to play nice with others."

He turned to look at Tender. "Agent Tender can you explain why you believe something is not right at St. Paul's?"

Tender Answers the Call

"First, I want to disclose that my mom was in this orphanage from a very early age until she was eighteen years old," Tender began. Then she proceeded to explain all the evidence we discovered, and why I wanted the FBI to start a case. Director Lance told Agent Sisson to get a team of agents assembled immediately. He added, "Let's get these girls home to Sister Mary Ellen."

When I asked him why he agreed to go forward with the case, the director said, "If an FBI agent brings a case before me, I almost always start a new case. The FBI never likes to take a chance that someone would be harmed if they denied a case. I hope that with you on the team, we will be able to close this case with a happy ending. So, let's get to work." I went over, thanked him again, and shook his hand.

On the way out, Agent Sisson was excited and promised to gather a team worthy of such a difficult case.

As we passed the front desk, Big John called out to Tender, "Come over and tell me about your case. When Tender explained about the missing girls, Big John got so angry. "Please find these girls, for all the missing girls in the world." he growled.

"We will." Tender replied. "Thanks for the rainbow lollipop."

"Hey, David Purdy, I saw you lick Agent Tender's lollipop." Big John pointed at David and said, "Agents only." We all laughed, but Big John yelled, "I'm not joking."

On the way home, I asked Tender, "Will Richard and Mary be at our house when we get there?"

"Not yet, but they'll come over as soon as school gets out," she replied.

David, who was not paying much attention, asked, "What is everyone hungry for? I'm starving. We never had lunch." I let Tender pick, and she wanted hot dogs. David got out the grill once we were home, and it wasn't too long before Mary and Richard were in the backyard.

Richard was excited when we told them that the FBI had approved our case and that we would start tomorrow. "Mary and I have discovered some very valuable information, and we can't wait to share it with you," he said in a rush.

Once we were all full of hot dogs, corn on the cob, and potato chips, we headed to our home investigation room.

THIRTEEN

Where Are the Sixty?

Richard began to tell us about their discovery. "Mary and I went to the library and investigated over nineteen orphanages across the country where girls live in a religious setting. We discovered over fifty-six girls have gone missing in the last four years, and fourteen of the orphanages had found those disappearances suspicious, now including St. Paul's. Almost all the schools had four girls go missing four months in a row, all during the same week of each month. Now all fifteen of the schools filed complaints with their local police."

"So, we have another fifty-six missing girls, not including the four from St. Paul's." I gasped.

"Yes, that is very concerning. And all these girls came from fifteen different states," Mary said. She twisted her hands in her lap.

"Well, now we know for sure we have a criminal enterprise crossing the country and kidnapping innocent girls. I believe it will be easy to track their movements, but I am worried about finding all these girls," Tender said seriously.

"Mary and Richard, would you please leave the room for one minute?" asked David. Once they left, he continued. "As our team leader, I would like to call a meeting to order."

"I second the motion." Tender, as vice president, liked making and seconding motions.

"I make a motion that we add Mary and Richard to our team at a wage of $2.00 an hour for each of them, as our investigative reporters, and give them 10 percent of any rewards we receive," David said.

"I second the motion," Tender said again.

"Very good. They will be paid from the business account once a month," David said as he called for a vote. "All in favor, thumbs-up for a yes."

We all agreed with a thumbs-up. David went out to the front porch and invited Mary and Richard back in.

Please sit down. "We have a proposal to offer you both," David said. "We were so impressed with your due diligence in investigating and reporting back to us. You are being offered a position on Team Purdy at a wage of $2.00 per working hour, with 10 percent of any rewards we receive. You don't have to say yes tonight. Think it over first."

They looked at each other and both shouted at the same time, "Yes!"

"Wait. Before we accept your answer, think it over and be prepared to tell us why you want to be on our team in the next forty-eight hours," said David. "We will have the contracts ready to sign on Friday night after pizza."

They were so excited that they hugged, and Richard gave Mary a kiss on the lips in front of us.

David yelled, "Hey! I never kissed a girl until I knew I was going to marry that girl."

Mary just smiled. "Dear brother, are you really expecting me to wait until someone asks me to marry him?"

"Of course not, but we do expect you to be careful," I said. David just shook his head.

The next morning, Tender was the first one up, as she loved to be prepared for her next adventure. David came over and gave his daughter a kiss on the cheek, like he did every morning. When Tender greeted him, she said, "Where is mom?" "She is not ready," David said, "Be careful, honey. She is not happy with her hair this morning."

"I heard that, David!" I stopped in the hall and gave him a threatening look.

"Sorry, dear. How foolish of me to try to understand your hair," teased David.

"Let's head over to the Eveready Diner. I am starved," said Tender. So off we drove in my Chevy. Tender liked my driving better because I don't speed through the yellow lights. David never stops for yellows but floors it instead. I would always tell him that it turned red before he was through, and he would respond that he was more than halfway. It is the only thing we disagree on. I even tell him that if anything were to happen to my little girl, I would be sure to teach him a lesson.

After breakfast, we headed to FBI headquarters. As we entered, Big John yelled, "Agent Tender, get over here." He knelt to look at Tender. "What case are you solving today? Is it the one with the four missing girls?"

"Actually, we have discovered an additional fifty-six girls from fourteen other orphanages that went missing." Tender put her hands on her hips.

"Tender, go get 'em, girl." Big John roared. Then he gave Tender her rainbow lollipop. David put his hands together as if he were begging, but John just repeated his catchphrase, "Agents only—but I will make you a deal. If you find all sixty of the girls, I will make one exception and give you one of my famous rainbow lollipops, which I have had made just for my special agents like Tender."

"Tender, I am counting on you. I need that lollipop," David begged.

Once we were in the elevator, Tender offered her dad a lick, and this time he took a bite. Tender had to grab it away from him.

As we entered the investigation room, Team Purdy took control. There were only six agents in the room, including Agent Sisson.

"Before we start, we have some new discoveries," I said. "Two of our new team members discovered that we are now looking for a total of sixty missing girls. Before we proceed, we need to speak to Director Lance."

Agent Sisson told all the agents to go back to their stations and return in one hour sharp. As we reached Director Lance's office, his secretary informed us he was in a meeting, and she had been given orders that he was not to be disturbed for any reason.

Agent Sisson whispered in Tender's ear. "You are the only one who can enter his office without getting in trouble, so run."

Tender ran over and opened his door. He looked up, and she saw him with the Secretary of the Navy. They both stood up in surprise just as his personal secretary was about to grab Tender, he waved her away. His secretary shut the door behind her with a frown.

The Secretary of the Navy came over to the intruder. "So, this is the famous Tender Purdy." he said.

"Nice to meet you in person, Mr. Secretary," Tender replied.

"How did you know who I was, Tender?" said Mr. Secretary.

"I read a lot," Tender said.

"This must be important, for you to enter during a closed-door meeting," replied Director Lance.

"It is sir." Tender went on to explain what her team had discovered. The Secretary was so upset that he thumped his fist on Director Lance's desk. "Director, I demand you put your best agents on this case immediately!" he shouted.

"Mr. Secretary, we already have our best agent on the case, and you are looking at her." replied Director Lance. "Tender, you go out and tell Agent Sisson he is to assemble the A-team for this case. One more thing—you are to tell no one who was in this meeting with me, understood?" ordered Director Lance.

"Yes, sir," said Tender, as she waved goodbye.

Tender, David, and I went to the cafeteria as

instructed by Agent Sisson, while he assembled the A-team. I asked Tender who had been in that meeting with Director Lance, but she refused to tell me, because she had been ordered to keep his identification a secret.

"Come on, at least tell us this: did you know who it was?" asked David.

I punched him in the arm. "David Purdy, you know better than to try to trick our daughter into disobeying an order."

"Sorry. You know how I hate it when I don't know everything my daughter knows." David grumbled. We both laughed.

Just then, an agent from the A-team came to get us. Tender, David, and I were surprised to see thirty agents anxious and excited to be working with us. I stood at the chalkboard as Tender laid out the case.

"To my surprise," Tender said, "we have sixty missing girls in fifteen states unaccounted for. Not one police department was willing to investigate, including the Lincoln Police department. It all started when my mom received a letter from Sister Mary Ellen. For those who are not familiar with my mom, she grew up in an orphanage, St. Paul's School for Girls. She was dropped off as a baby, and she never knew her last name. Mom, please explain what the letter contained."

"The letter from Sister Mary Ellen explained how four girls went missing in four months, during the first week of each month. Sister Mary Ellen was concerned because typically only one girl a year runs away, and they always leave a goodbye note. But this time, the girls left no note; they just went missing. My sister-in-law, Mary, and her boyfriend, Richard, discovered that the same situation has happened in a total of fifteen states, including North Dakota. So, what we know is that we have sixty missing girls. I refer to Tender to explain what happened," I concluded.

"Here is what I believe happened. This is an organized crime ring targeting minor children. First, they purchase a food delivery service, which delivers only to religious orphanages for girls. They find girls who were delivered at birth with no last name. My mom will explain," said Tender, nodding to me.

"I was dropped off at the orphanage as a baby, and since I had no last name, I was given the name of Smith. Every girl that is dropped off with no last name is given a common last name like Smith. Each girl that was taken had no last name. This makes it almost impossible to find them, as Tender will explain." I motioned for Tender to continue.

"We believe that the girls who are taken are

told by the kidnappers that their birth parents have been found. They are told that they were kidnapped at birth and that their parents have never stopped looking for them. All the criminals must do is convince the parents, grandparents, or other family members of missing children that they have located their missing child. They then research what the missing girl might look like, based on the other children in the family. They are probably basing the reward amounts on what kind of area the parents reside in. The more affluent the area is, the higher the payout. Most families are willing to do anything these criminals require. My estimate is they had over one hundred families willing to pay any price for the return of their daughter. All the criminals needed to do was watch a child.

"I am going to give out assignments, which need to be completed as soon as possible," said Tender. "First, Agent Sisson, please pair up agents to head out to the fifteen targeted schools. Once the teams are there, they are to get the names, ages, and photos of the four girls removed, as well as any description of employees working as food delivery workers."

Since agents always work in pairs, the first assignment began quickly. Once each team leader was given his or her assigned school, the agents headed to their lockers to retrieve their overnight bags. Then they reported to the transport room, where Agent Carol Owens either gave them the keys to a vehicle or assigned them to report to the airport. Six teams were given a vehicle, and eight teams were to report to the FBI air hangar, where the teams would be dropped off in eight different states. Each were given a pickup time later the following day. All agents were to report back to headquarters on the morning of the third day.

Tender told David to collect Mary and Richard, along with their notes. Their assignment would be to contact the schools who reported the missing girls and find out if they had noticed new workers on the food crew in their school. Once they could find where the kidnappers might be working, they were to report back to her quickly.

Agent Sisson assigned Agent William Bello to go with David. As they were about to leave, Tender yelled, "Wait! One more important note: when Mary arrives, have her do the talking with the schools. If need be, have her explain she was a new hire and forgot where she was to meet and what day to report. I don't want the school to panic."

"Okay, boss," replied Agent Bello.

"Agent Bello, my dad will have to convince Mary to lie, as she may not be willing to do that. Explain to her it is okay to deceive in police work if it helps us to find the kidnappers," said Tender.

"I will convince her," David replied.

"Next, Agent Sisson, please get every young female agent you have working in this building to report up here in thirty minutes. Mom, you need to pick the youngest-looking agent you can find." Both Agent Sisson and I were confused by Tender's request.

Agent Sisson reported back in less than thirty minutes with some forty agents. He was as proud as a peacock. "I looked the agents over and found two with baby-looking faces," he said.

Tender proceeded to ask them questions. "Do either of you have a black belt in karate?" They both responded with a yes.

"Well, then, I have few questions for you both," I said. "Your names, how old you are, how long you have been an agent, and if any of you have been in action as of yet," I drilled them.

The first agent spoke up. "My name is Lisa O'Brien, I am twenty-two, I am just finishing my first year, and I have never been in action. I am small but tough, and I can't wait to prove myself."

"My name is Carrie Collins, I am twenty-six, I have been an agent for four years, and I have been in the field for the past year," said the second agent.

"Very good. I will need both of you; however, this first assignment requires Agent Collins," Tender said. "You will need to infiltrate the school as a new student. We will arrange for you to enter as a seventeen-year-old. You look young; how tall are you?"

"I am four feet, nine inches, and I weigh one hundred pounds," she replied.

One of the taller agents, Wanda Wallach, was at least six feet tall, with a strong face; she looked tough. Tender motioned her over. "Once we have the location that the kidnappers are working from, you ladies will go into action. The FBI will arrest one of the girls in the crew, leaving them one girl short. You will need to stage a fight in front of the kidnappers and convince them you are a criminal. This is how your fight will happen. Outside, in front of the kidnappers, Agent Wallach will try to snatch a purse from Agent Collins, who will be posing as a student. Agent Collins will run after her as fast as she can, but Agent Wallach is faster. Agent Wallach will duck into a bar, where a fight ensues. Agent Collins will be roughed up, but she will escape with her purse and run out of the bar."

Tender then continued, "Most likely, the kidnappers will ask you what happened, Agent Wallach. You will reply that you don't want to talk about it.

They will remark that it looks like you are not a very good thief. You will say you're having an off day. We are sure they will then offer you a position on their crew. You respond, 'How much does it pay?' Whatever they say, tell them you want double the amount. If they say, 'That's all it pays, take it or leave it,' you accept and respond, 'Can't blame a girl for trying.'"

"Tender, won't they think their missing girl will return?" asked Agent Wallach.

"No, she will have left a note stating she is quitting, and that they shouldn't worry because she will never snitch, as it would mean jail time for her," Tender reassured her.

Agent Sisson told Agents Collins and Wallach to report to the gym for training. They were to explain to the trainer that their fight needed to look real, including real punches when in the bar.

Tender told me that she was tired and hungry, and we left for the cafeteria.

Meanwhile, David had left with Agent Bello to collect Mary and Richard, who were excited to leave school early. With all their hard work in hand, they arrived at FBI headquarters. At the front desk, Big John had them fill out the check-in forms. "Mary Purdy how are you related to Agent Tender Purdy?" he asked.

"Tender is my niece," she replied.

"That would make you Detective David's sister. Richard Harris, what is your business at FBI headquarters?" asked Big John, looking Richard up and down suspiciously.

"I am part of the Purdy's team," Richard replied with a nervous smile.

David and Agent Bello escorted Mary and Richard upstairs. We greeted them, and within ten minutes we were heading to the seventh floor, where we entered a room with over fifty desks and agents just waiting for instructions. David briefed all the agents on the dialogue they would need to use to get the information that would lead to the location of the kidnappers. We needed to follow up on 250 possible leads, which would require five calls per agent.

After many calls, Mary pointed to a hot lead from Agent Kim O'Rourke. First, she got a positive response from an orphanage about having a new food crew. Agent O'Rourke put the call on speaker. "Mrs. Marie Pavan, thank you for that information. I need to find my sister, as my mother has taken ill. All she told me was that a food delivery company had hired her to work at a children's home in Albuquerque, New Mexico," said Kim O'Rourke.

"Yes, we are using the same company, except

all new workers showed up this week," Mrs. Pavan answered.

"What days do they deliver?" Agent O'Rourke followed up.

"Mondays and Thursdays," replied Mrs. Pavan.

"What time can I catch my sister? Or could you share their address with me?" pressed Agent O'Rourke.

"Wait, let me see where we mail the payments," Mrs. Pavan said helpfully. She quickly found the address and gave it to Agent O'Rourke, who wrote it down.

"Thank you so much. I will hope to thank you in person soon," finished Agent O'Rourke.

All the agents were required to check in three times a day unless they received the code they were given to come home. The code was, "On your way home, bring me some golden yellow apples." After the conversation between Agent O'Rourke and Mrs. Pavan, Tender gave the code for agents to return.

By early morning, every agent was waiting for Tender to give the orders. Tender spoke plainly to every agent about what they needed to do to stop this criminal enterprise. "If we fail to cut the head off the snake, this organization will just set up again in a year or so. I believe the head criminal has never been seen by the middlemen or women.

It's important that we catch that person. It will be up to Agent Wanda Wallach, our inside agent, to discover who is at the top. We will trail the middle person back to the leader. We were lucky we found the crew on call eighty-seven."

We headed home for the evening, but we planned to use the FBI as our base once the agents started with the arrests. Once we arrived the next morning, we remained on duty for seven days, taking cat naps all week. Only Tender had a bedroom set up so she could get a good night's sleep.

Every agent went above and beyond the call of duty. It was important to everyone that every criminal be arrested.

One night I heard Tender crying, and I immediately ran into her temporary bedroom. When I entered her room, she was crying hysterically. I rushed over and hugged her. "Tender, it's all right. I am here," I said comfortingly.

"I was frightened that you and Dad left me, and you no longer wanted me." Tender said between sniffles. Then she started to cry again.

"Tender, I have never loved any one person more than I love you. Don't tell Dad, but I love you even more than him," I said with a smile.

David stuck his head into the open door. "I heard that. And I knew a long time ago that Mom loves you more than me," he replied. "In fact, like Mom, I loved you from the first day we met," said David, with a big smile. "But, Tender, why would you think that we didn't want you anymore?" David asked as he sat on the edge of her bed.

"I was confused when I woke up in this strange room, and you weren't with me, so I was afraid that, like my first mommy, you left me too." Tender said. She clung to me and sniffled.

"Tender, your first mommy didn't leave you; she is watching over you in heaven. And we would never leave you." I said, wiping her face with a tissue.

Tender smiled and gave David and me a big hug and held us both for the longest time. "I love you, Mom; I love you, Dad. But I don't want to sleep in this scary room ever again," she begged.

"Tender do you know where we are?" David asked.

"Yes, Dad I do now; we are at the FBI headquarters, Tender remembered.

"Tender, if we ever have to sleep here again, I will sleep with you, all right?" I said.

"Okay, but do we have the sixty missing girls?"

"Not yet, but due to the good work done by the FBI and state police, we have made all the arrests except the snake in this kidnapping case," I reported.

"You will never guess in a thousand years who the snake is." David teased.

"Dad, you know me better than that. I know who it is," Tender said.

"Tender, if you know who it is, I will admit you are the best detective in the world." said David.

"Even better than Sherlock Holmes?" Tender asked.

"Even better than Sherlock Holmes, your favorite detective," David and I laughed.

"It's Chief Beck," Tender said.

"What." David jumped to his feet and smacked his forehead with his right hand. "How could you possibly know that?"

"One night in my sleep, I remembered something was wrong when we went to see him. He had no interest in finding the missing girls, no matter what evidence we presented. Remember when we tried to convince him that there was a sting operation taking place all over the country? He brushed it off as just a bunch of runaways. I also noticed on his desk a check for $5,000. Finally, when we pleaded with Chief Beck to open the case and he refused, I knew he was the snake." Tender smiled and said, "Go ahead and say it, Dad."

"Tender Louise, you are a better detective than

the fictional character Sherlock Holmes." exclaimed David.

Just then, Agent Sisson walked in. "Tender, I agree with that, although I don't know why I am saying it," Agent Sisson said.

"Agent Sisson, Tender figured out that Chief Beck is the snake." David said proudly.

"Of course, she did." Agent Sisson said. "And Director Lance wants a meeting in the cafeteria for updates and breakfast."

As we entered the cafeteria, every agent stood and clapped for Team Purdy. Tender turned and went over to her favorite agent. "Big John, I request your presence next to me at table six," she said with a smile.

"Tender there is no room at that table." Big John protested.

Tender grabbed his enormous hand and walked him over to table six, while he held his food tray with his other hand. "Would all the agents at table six please look this way?" Most of the agents had their heads down eating, but they all looked up at Tender. "You know I love every one of you, but none more than Big John. So, I need to ask someone to volunteer his seat. I would consider it a big favor." Tender gave the agents a puppy-dog look, and almost every agent stood up. Tender tapped the agent next to her seat and thanked him for giving up his seat.

Big John and Tender were talking and enjoying themselves when Director Lance began to brief the room. "The kidnappers have admitted only to taking the four girls from St. Paul's School for Girls. So, Tender, we are stuck."

Big John lifted Tender on top of the cafeteria table so she could talk to everyone. "Thank you, Agent Riley," Tender said. "We know that all the girls range from twelve to seventeen years old. We need every agent searching for missing babies taken as far back as seventeen years ago to five years ago. We will need forty-eight agents to call every state police chief, asking for this information. Once you find the family members who have lost a child, contact them to see if their child has been returned. The child I most need to find is the deaf girl, Vicky Smith," Tender explained.

Then Tender said, "Director Lance, I would like Big John working on this case, please."

"Tender, you can request any agent on a case in which you are the lead agent," Director Lance replied. Then Director Lance spoke to the agents in the room. "This is going to be an emotional upheaval to the children and family members who think their child has been found. When you receive confirmation of a girl that has been found, I will send two of our best agents who act in a professional manner and specialize in family matters. They will gently inform the families of the kidnapping and scam. Any questions?" asked Director Lance.

"Director Lance, may I suggest that once the families are informed, an adoption packet should be given to all these disappointed parents and children who believe they found their family. It will be heartbreaking for them to lose a loved one again," I put in. "And Tender also suggested that the adoption should not take more than thirty days. Would you see if that is possible?" I asked.

Director Lance liked this suggestion and promised he would investigate it. Then he ordered Agent Sisson to get his forty-eight best agents started on finding these missing girls. He was also concerned about Tender's safety until Chief Beck was in custody. He appointed John Riley to watch Tender day and night.

"Yes, sir," Big John replied.

"David and Elaine Purdy have also been ordered to shadow Tender until Chief Beck is in custody," said Director Lance. "I was informed that his wife, Carol Ann Beck, is in custody but not talking."

"Is it really necessary having Agent Riley be on Tender's protection detail, since David and I are detectives?" I asked.

Big John jumped up and banged the table so hard the other end lifted up a few inches. "Yes! When I was younger, I was on the presidential detail. I protected several different Presidents of the United States. If I was willing to give my life to protect someone whom I didn't care for, how much more would I give my life to protect Tender, whom I love." Big John exclaimed.

Tender grabbed Big John's hand and squeezed it.

"Nothing more to do here, so we will give you a ride to our home, Big John," David said.

"One more request, Agent Sisson," Tender asked, motioning for him to come over.

"You name it, boss," he said, bending down to her level.

"I would like to speak to the agents who will be delivering the news to the parents," said Tender.

"I will make sure they speak to you. Meanwhile, wait here in the cafeteria for Agent Riley's instructions," Agent Sisson told her. He straightened up and walked out of the room.

Then Big John spoke to us about Tender's safety. "Please eat now, because Tender will not be going out to eat anytime soon," he said.

Since we had just had breakfast, we weren't very hungry, but we decided to get some more food anyway. David got a steak, I got my favorite salad, and Tender got pizza. To my surprise, Big John would not eat until we got Tender home safe and sound.

Big John gathered several agents who were on Tender's protective duty around our table. "What I am about to tell you makes me very angry," said Big John. "Everyone on this duty, listen up closely to what I am about to say. I am allowing Tender to stay and be a part of the discussion. I am about to read a note we received in the mail."

Big John was so upset as he read that his face flushed.

To all the losers at the FBI, this is Chief Beck. You will never find me, as I was in the Special Forces and can hide out of sight for years. I know who caused me to be in this predicament—it was Tender Purdy. I will only make this offer once to Director Lance. You either grant my wife and me a full pardon, or I will kill Tender Purdy. There is not an agent in the FBI who can stop me. You have twenty-four hours to give me your answer.

I gasped for air and put my hand over my mouth.

Big John said to the agents, "Stand and raise your right hand and repeat after me: 'As an FBI agent, I will always guard and protect Tender Purdy, even to the loss of my life, so help me God.' "

Every agent stood up and repeated the oath, including David.

"Very good. The following procedures will be in place," said Big John. "Whenever we are on the move, Tender's code name will be Fishhook."

Tender yelled, "Fishhook?" No way."

I replied, "How about 'Eveready'?"

David looked at Tender questioningly. Tender nodded her head in agreement.

"Okay, then, Eveready it is," Big John agreed. "Every time Tender exits a building, I will lead her in the middle, with an agent on each side and one in the back," Big John ordered. "All you Purdys will travel in an FBI bulletproof caravan and wear a bulletproof vest. I will also assign extra coverage outside your house," Big John continued.

Tender spoke up. "To protect all my agents, each agent will bring decoy agents. Put one in the driver's seat and one in the passenger seat when you exit the vehicle and try not to be seen. If you haven't been trained in Special Forces, you will lose the battle unless you follow my orders," Tender spoke.

"Once we know Chief Beck is making his move, we will allow him to enter the house. He is already hiding out, and he will find a way in. My plan only

Tender Answers the Call

works if you do as I say," ordered Big John in a stern voice.

It took a few days to get everything ready. On day three everyone got in their armored vehicles and headed out. Big John carried a dummy looking like Tender into the house, with agents on each side and one in the back. They thought she would be safest lying on the couch facing back. Three agents were always close by Tender.

Time went by quickly, and soon Tender had fallen asleep at the safehouse. At about 3 AM, Chief Beck entered quietly through a side window. He saw what he thought was Tender sleeping on the couch and prepared to shoot, first at the agents and then at Tender. Before he could shoot, the lights went on, and he was surrounded by twenty agents. Not wanting to be captured, he was about to shoot his way out when all twenty agents ended the threat. The trap had worked.

David received the call and yelled, "They got him."

I ran over to David and hugged him. "Agent Riley, is he ever going to be able to harm Tender?" I asked.

"No!"

I was relieved that Tender didn't find out what happened until the morning.

"Good morning, Mom. Am I safe?" Tender asked.

"Yes, forever," I said.

We headed to the FBI building to have breakfast at the cafeteria. On the way there, I asked Tender, "Are you okay, darling? I am worried that you were traumatized by the whole affair."

"Mom, I don't know why, but I found it exciting. I also felt that you and Dad were concerned, which helped keep me calm. I knew no one was going to even get close to me," Tender replied.

"I also found it exciting, and I'm relieved Big John's plan worked," I said.

Just then, we entered the cafeteria, and every agent stood and clapped. Big John gave Tender a big hug. Tender asked Big John to put her on top of the table so she could address the agents.

"I am so proud of you all. Thank you for saving me from Chief Beck." Tender looked around the room and thanked everyone by name and told them she loved them all. "Are all my agents alive and well?" Tender asked.

"Yes, they are all well, thanks to your plan. A few decoy agents are going to need to be sewn back together," replied Agent Sisson.

"Tender, because your house is a crime scene, the FBI has arranged for you to stay at one of our safe houses," explained Director Lance.

"When will I know about the missing girls?" Tender was anxious to know.

"We have some good reports, and we have located about half of them. Starting Monday, we will be sending Agent Anna Gravel and Agent Michelle Medeiros to gently inform the families about the scam played on them," said Director Lance.

"Director Lance, before they start, I want to instruct them, please," Tender requested.

"Yes, we had planned for you to guide them," said Director Lance.

After our breakfast, everyone headed home for some rest, as it had been a long night. Tender, David, and I headed to the safe house. Once we arrived there, four agents stationed themselves outside to guard us in the way Big John had instructed agents to protect us.

"Why is that necessary?" David asked.

"When an agent's life has been threatened, it is procedure that we treat the threat as ongoing for two weeks," replied Agent Lawson, one of the four agents stationed at the safe house.

"That makes sense. I'm glad the FBI has this safety protocol," said David.

The safe house was beautiful; it was a cozy cabin and had a country feel. Wood beams cradled the cathedral ceilings. As we toured the cabin, everything smelled like cedar.

"Tender, what kind of wood is this kitchen?" I asked.

"The kitchen is rosewood, and it has marble countertops," Tender replied.

Agent Lawson remarked, "I always wondered what kind of tree these beautiful cabinets were made of. Thank you, Tender."

"You're welcome," Tender replied cheerfully.

Just then, there was a knock on the door, and in came Agent Gravel and Agent Medeiros.

"Good day, ladies. That was quick," I said.

"Is this the famous Tender Purdy? "We are so excited to be working on your team," said Agent Gravel.

"Tender, we are here to be instructed on how to handle the situation with the families," Agent Gravel said.

"Yes, please sit down," Tender replied. "As an orphan for eighteen years, my mom never had a last name, just like these girls. Her whole childhood, she prayed that someday a family member would show up and reveal her identity. I want you to first approach these families in private without the girls present. Then ask them how they feel about having their child back."

Agent Gravel interrupted, "Should we introduce ourselves as FBI agents?"

"Yes, sorry; I should have mentioned that first. When you first enter, you will introduce yourselves as agents, and then ask to speak alone. Be gentle as you ask them how it feels to have their child back. Do not interrupt them if they are happy to talk. Then ask them if, in order to keep custody, they might have to adopt their child, would they be willing to do so?" Tender spoke softly. "They will respond, 'Why would we need to adopt our own child?' At this time, you will need to explain what might have happened. Explain that you are going to do a blood test on the child and on both parents. It may be possible they are the parents. If a problem develops, hand them the adoption papers and let them know the government has green-lit a thirty-day approval. But if they resist strongly, you will then need to put on your FBI demeanor and show them the court order to remove the child until the adoption is settled. They will cooperate or risk the chance of losing the child for a few nights," said Tender.

"If they say they would not want to adopt the child, just show the court order and remove the child," I said. "After they agree that they would adopt her, one agent will spend some time with the girl in private, preferably in the backyard alone, take a blood sample, and ask questions: 'Are you happy? How do you like living here? Are you making friends?' The other agent will ask the family to remain inside with her. This is a good time to ask the family members questions. How is the child doing in school? Has she made any friends? Does she seem happy? Has she adjusted well? And most important, when did you receive the child?" Tender said.

Agent Medeiros took notes, which pleased Tender.

"Finally, show them a picture of Mrs. Beck and ask them if this is the woman who brought them the child. Then ask them how much they paid her." Tender concluded.

"I want you to contact us daily on this FBI line." I said as I handed Agent Medeiros the number.

"I am especially concerned about Vicky Smith; she is deaf, and I have a bad feeling about this girl's safety," Tender injected.

"Tender, we will follow your instruction to the letter," said Agent Gravel.

"May God be with you both," I said. Tender gave them both a hug.

The agents had sixty folders, each containing a history of one of the missing girls. After they left, I said, "Tender, that was amazing, but we are exhausted and need to get some sleep." I informed

Tender that FBI Agent Dana-Lee Jenson would be doing the cooking and would watch Tender when David and I were not around. She carried a gun in a shoulder holster. I was told she was the best woman marksman in the FBI, and she was tough, like me.

After several days of being cooped up, and with many good reports coming in from Agents Gravel and Medeiros, we were ready to go home. Tender was also ready to go back to school. One morning, Agent Sisson stopped by.

"Good morning, Purdys. We have not picked up any chatter about Tender anywhere, so we feel it is safe to send you home," said Agent Sisson.

"Can we bring Dana-Lee with us? She is such a good cook," I asked.

"I am sure she would love to, but we have another assignment for her," he laughed. Tender went over and gave Agent Dana-Lee a hug.

"Before you go home, Director Lance would like to see all of you," he said.

Tender thanked all the agents who had been protecting her at the safe house, and then we got into the FBI vehicle and headed to headquarters. We entered Director Lance's office, who was glad to see us safe.

"Agent Tender, after one week of meeting with the families, we have some good results," said

Director Lance. "Agent Gravel and Agent Medeiros have contacted fifteen families. So far, all the families are going to adopt the girls who were with them, and none were the biological parents," Director Lance continued.

"Director Lance, was Vicky Smith among the girls they found?" Tender inquired.

"No, sorry, but we are going to find her," he replied.

On our way home we dropped Tender off at school and went in to see Principal Adler. "Welcome back, Tender it is good to see you. Mrs. Purdy, tell me—did you solve your case?" she asked, wondering what the case was about.

"Yes, the FBI has located fifteen missing girls, and they have forty-five more to locate," Tender informed her.

"Did you find the bad guys?" asked Mrs. Adler.

"Yes, we caught them all," I said.

"Well, good for you. We are so proud of you, Tender," she said with a smile.

As Tender was on her way to her class, all the children wanted to question Tender about her case. She would not discuss the case with the older students until she was satisfied all the girls were safe. "Sorry, but we are still working on it; all I can say is that all the bad people are in jail," said Tender.

Everyone was patting her on the back. Tender liked the attention.

David and I headed home to freshen up, and then we drove to police headquarters. We reported to Chief Purdy, who had been filled in on all that was going on. David had been speaking to him daily. He also told us he had had several men posted outside the FBI cabin all week to keep an eye on Tender.

Then Chief Purdy said, "Tonight is the meeting at the city hall before the city council, to present our case for the special force."

"We will be there," David replied.

David and I spent all day looking at our cold case. Before the end of the day, we both left early to get Tender from school. She was excited to go to her first city council meeting.

When we got home, Mary and Richard were waiting outside the house on the porch.

"Well, how did we do? Tell us everything!" shouted Richard.

David ordered pizza, and then he went to freshen up. Tender told them how everything went and that she had had a threat on her life.

"We knew something was up. The FBI was here for a week, and the cleaning crew just finished up yesterday. Was someone killed in the house?" asked Mary.

"Yes, Allen Beck, the former police chief from Lincoln," Tender reported.

"Was he the snake?" asked Richard.

"Yes, and it shows crime never pays," I said. "We are so proud of your contribution in helping us discover not just four kidnapped girls, but sixty. The good news is that we have located fifteen girls. They are also going to be adopted by the families," I informed them. Then I invited them to attend the council meeting that night.

"Yes, we would love to attend," Richard said. "Oh, sorry, Mary. I didn't mean to speak for both of us. Mary, would you like to attend?

"Yes, I would love to go." Mary said with a smile.

As David was coming down the hall, the pizza was delivered. After we ate, Tender and I went to freshen up. Then we were all off to the meeting.

On our way there, Tender explained to Mary and Richard. "I have a job for you both, and it is going to be difficult. You remember what we know about Vicky Smith?"

"Yes, she is the deaf girl, right?" said Mary.

"She was the young girl Elaine helped with her homework when she was at St. Paul's," said Richard, who had a very good memory, though not as good as Tender.

"Well, I need you to find her, because she is deaf,

and I have a bad feeling about her. I believe she is in trouble and is crying out," said Tender.

"Where do we start?" asked Richard.

"Go to the library and find every school for deaf children in the United States. Then contact them and ask if they have enrolled any new students in the last few months," said Tender.

"Tender, if they are deaf, how will they answer the phone?" asked Mary.

"Most will have an office administrator who can hear as well as use sign language," Tender explained.

"Okay, but what if they don't employ such a person? What then?" Richard asked.

"We will contact the local FBI office, and they will send an agent who knows sign language," Tender said.

Just then, we pulled up to city hall. When we entered the building, everyone wanted to know what had been going on at our house. I was not willing to say too much; I would only say that we couldn't talk about an ongoing case.

FOURTEEN

Where Is Victory Smith?

The only matter on the agenda was the new police task force. The mayor called the meeting to order, and then Chief Purdy was asked to come forward. "Chief Purdy, thank you for your service to Bismarck," said the mayor.

"Thank you, Mr. Mayor. As of right now, we have forty-six unsolved cases, which include everything from murder to missing children, bank robbers, car thief rings, attacks on the elderly, larceny, arsonists, and hit-and-runs with death resulting. I have put together a task force to work on solving these unsolved cases. I have the task force with me tonight if you have any questions for them."

Chief Purdy motioned for us to come forward, and we all stood up before the council. I think Tender enjoyed her time in the spotlight. The

Tender Answers the Call

president of the council, Scott Westfall, asked all the questions.

"What makes you the best team to lead this new task force?" he asked.

"We have FBI Agent Tender Purdy, and she is as smart as they come," responded David.

"Is this young lady going to lead the task force at her age?" questioned Councilman Westfall, eyebrows raised.

The chief spoke up. "No, Detective Purdy will lead the team. Tender is the brains behind uncovering some of the details that will lead to arrests. She has already solved cases for the FBI. Because of her, a five-year-old boy who was abducted from his yard was recovered the very same day."

"May I ask Tender a question?" asked Councilman Westfall.

I nodded yes.

"Tender, if you are working on a task force, how will you attend school?" he asked with a frown.

"I attend a Montessori School, which has a more flexible schedule," replied Tender.

"So, what did you learn last year, and what grade are you in?" pressed the councilman.

"I am not sure what grade I am in," responded Tender calmly.

"How is that possible?!" demanded the councilman.

"All I can tell you is in the last year and a half, I graduated from law school," confirmed Tender.

"That's impossible at your age!" blurted out the councilman.

Tender pulled out a card from her pocket and handed it to me. I passed it to Councilman Westfall for him to examine. Tender continued, "I have passed the bar. I am the youngest lawyer in North Dakota."

"Amazing. Do you have to attend classes every day?" asked Councilman Westfall.

"I like school, so I do attend most days. However, if someone in your family went missing, I would have to miss school to help either the FBI or the police find them," replied Tender.

"Thank you very much, Tender. We have enjoyed speaking with you," Councilman Westfall concluded.

"If you ever need an attorney, give me a call," Tender said with a smile. Everyone laughed.

After the questions, the council went into their private chambers to decide the outcome, as this was the only matter on the agenda tonight. After about thirty minutes, they returned and cast their vote. The entire council voted to approve the request for the task force, pending a budget meeting next month. Chief Purdy had already submitted his budget, but it was up to the council's discretion to use excess funds in the budget.

After the meeting, Chief Purdy thanked them all. "Tender, you did wonderful."

"Thank you, Uncle Frank," Tender smiled.

"Tomorrow, you all need to report to FBI headquarters first thing in the morning. You are on loan again," Chief Purdy nodded at us.

The next morning, we had breakfast at 7 AM at the Eveready Diner, and then we reported to the FBI at 8 AM. Tender enjoyed entering the headquarters and being addressed as Agent Tender. At the front desk, Big John told us to report to Director Lance's office.

Director Lance got right to the point. "I knew you would like to hear the good news about our ongoing case. We are pleased to report we now have located thirty-two of the girls. Thirty of them have requested to be adopted by their new parents. The other two have asked to be returned to the school they came from. One of the male parents has been charged with a crime. If David would like more information, we can speak in private later on," reported Director Lance.

Tender spoke up. "Any word on Victory Smith?" she asked.

"Sorry, Tender; she is not on the list of the

thirty-two. Nevertheless, we are so proud of Team Purdy. Thank you for all your work on this case. The agents are really enjoying finding these missing girls," Director Lance concluded.

***

A few weeks went by, and we hadn't heard any more news on the missing girls. Then one day, we were told to come to FBI headquarters and report to Director Lance.

When we arrived, Director Lance greeted us and said, "The reason I asked you here is because we have located fifty-nine of the sixty girls. The good news is that forty-five of them remain with their new parents. Fourteen of the older girls wanted to be returned to their orphanages. David, I would like to speak to you privately so I can explain about Vicky Smith."

David asked him to please explain to all of us, as he knew Tender would want to be informed.

"Very well," said Director Lance. "Tender, I am sorry, but we were unable to find Vicky Smith. I must also tell you that I may now close the case."

Tender started to cry as we left to go home. Tender continued to be so upset in the car that we decided not to bring her to school. David headed to work, and I stayed home to comfort Tender.

Tender Answers the Call

"Mom," Tender asked tearfully, "do you think we'll ever find Victory Smith?"

"I don't know, darling," I told her. "But if anyone can, I'm sure —Team Purdy can!"

*Find out what happened to Vicky Smith
in the next volume of the Tender Purdy Mysteries.
This is not the end but just the beginning of
the Tender Purdy Mysteries!*

Tender Purdy and the Top-Secret Case!

About the Author

Richard P. Harrington grew up in the inner city in Providence, Rhode Island. Struggling through school and graduating with only a fifth-grade education made writing difficult. Richard worked for many years as a builder and cabinet maker before pursuing his life-long dream of writing mysteries. In 2021 Richard began dreaming each night about a little girl named Tender Purdy. His story comes to life as he uses real life events to write his intriguing stories.

Made in the USA
Middletown, DE
21 September 2024